LEGENDS OF CHIMA™

Yannick Grotholt – Writer

Comicon – Artist

New York

LEGO CHIMA Graphic Novels Available from PAPERCUTZ™

Coming Soon!

LEGO
LEGENDS OF
CHIMA
ALL-NEW GRAPHIC NOVEL SERIES!
HIGH RISK!
YANNICK GROTHOLT
COMICON
PAPERCUTZ

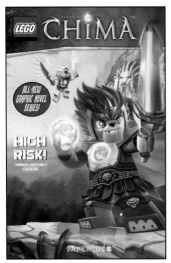

Graphic Novel #1
"High Risk!"

LEGO
LEGENDS OF
CHIMA
THE RIGHT DECISION
YANNICK GROTHOLT
COMICON
PAPERCUTZ

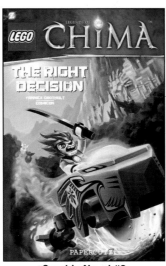

Graphic Novel #2
"The Right Decision"

LEGO
LEGENDS OF
CHIMA
CHI QUEST!
YANNICK
GROTHOLT
COMICON
PAPERCUTZ

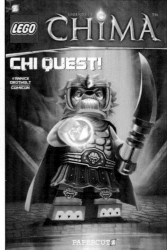

Graphic Novel #3
"CHI Quest!"

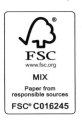

LEGO LEGENDS OF CHIMA graphic novels are available for $7.99 in paperback, $12.99 hardcover. Available from booksellers everywhere. You can also order online from Papercutz.com. Or call 1-800-886-1223, Monday through Friday, 9-5 EST. MC, Visa, and AmEx accepted. To order by mail, please add $4.00 for postage and handling for first book ordered, $1.00 for each additional book and make check payable to NBM Publishing. Send to: Papercutz, 160 Broadway, Suite 700, East Wing, New York, NY 10038.

LEGO LEGENDS OF CHIMA graphic novels are also available digitally wherever e-books are sold.

Papercutz.com

LEGENDS OF CHIMA
#2 "The Right Decision"

Yannick Grotholt – Writer
Comicon – Artist
Tom Orzechowski – Letterer
Max Gartman – Editorial Intern
Beth Scorzato – Production Coordinator
Michael Petranek – Editor
Jim Salicrup
Editor-in-Chief

ISBN: 978-1-62991-074-1 paperback edition
ISBN: 978-1-62991-075-8 hardcover edition

Printed in Canada
August 2014 by Friesens Printing
1 Printer Way
Altona, MB R0G 0B0

Papercutz books may be purchased for business or promotional use. For information on bulk purchases please contact Macmillan Corporate and Premium Sales Department at (800) 221-7945 x5442.

Distributed by Macmillan
First Papercutz Printing

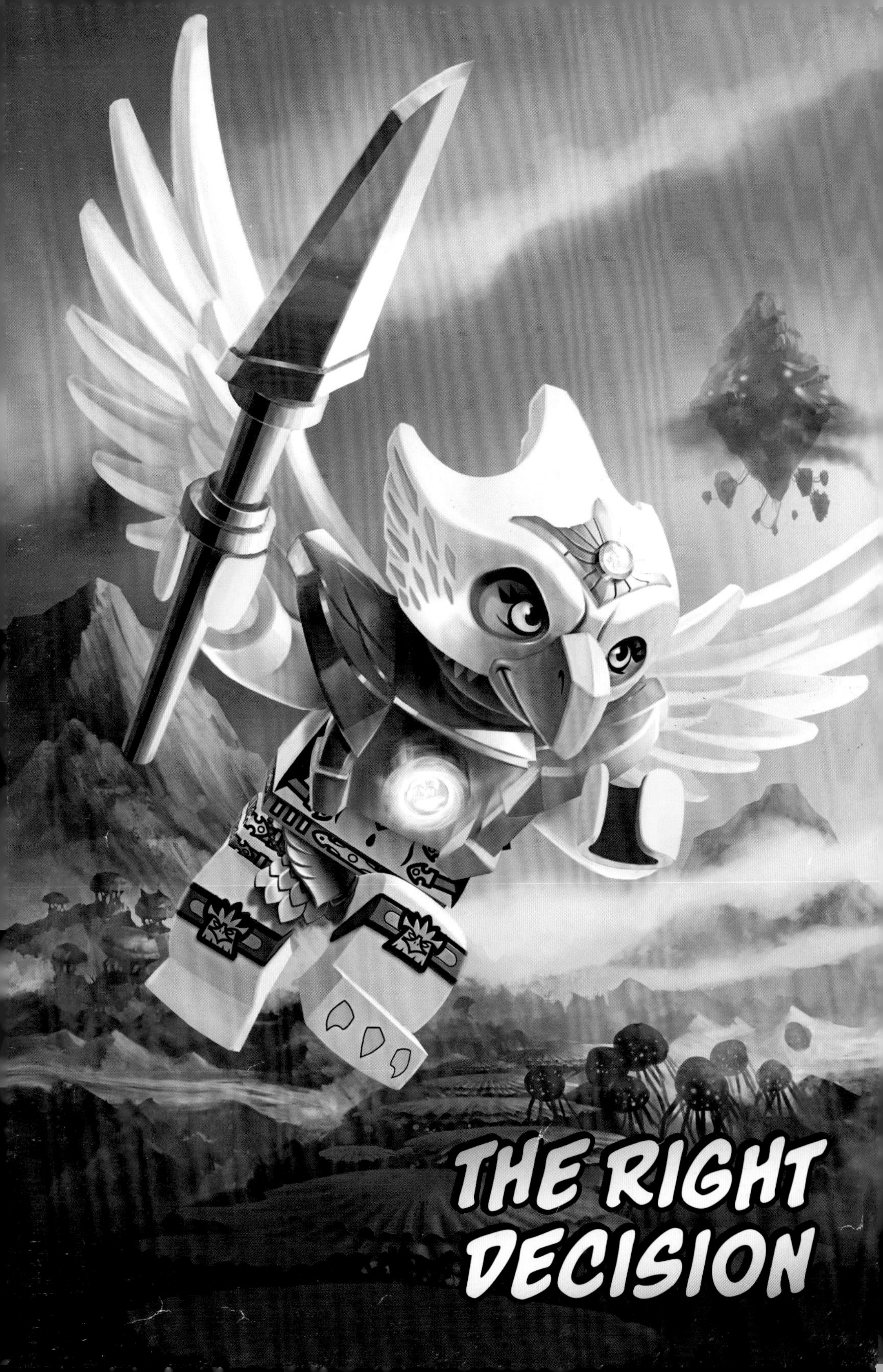

THE RIGHT DECISION

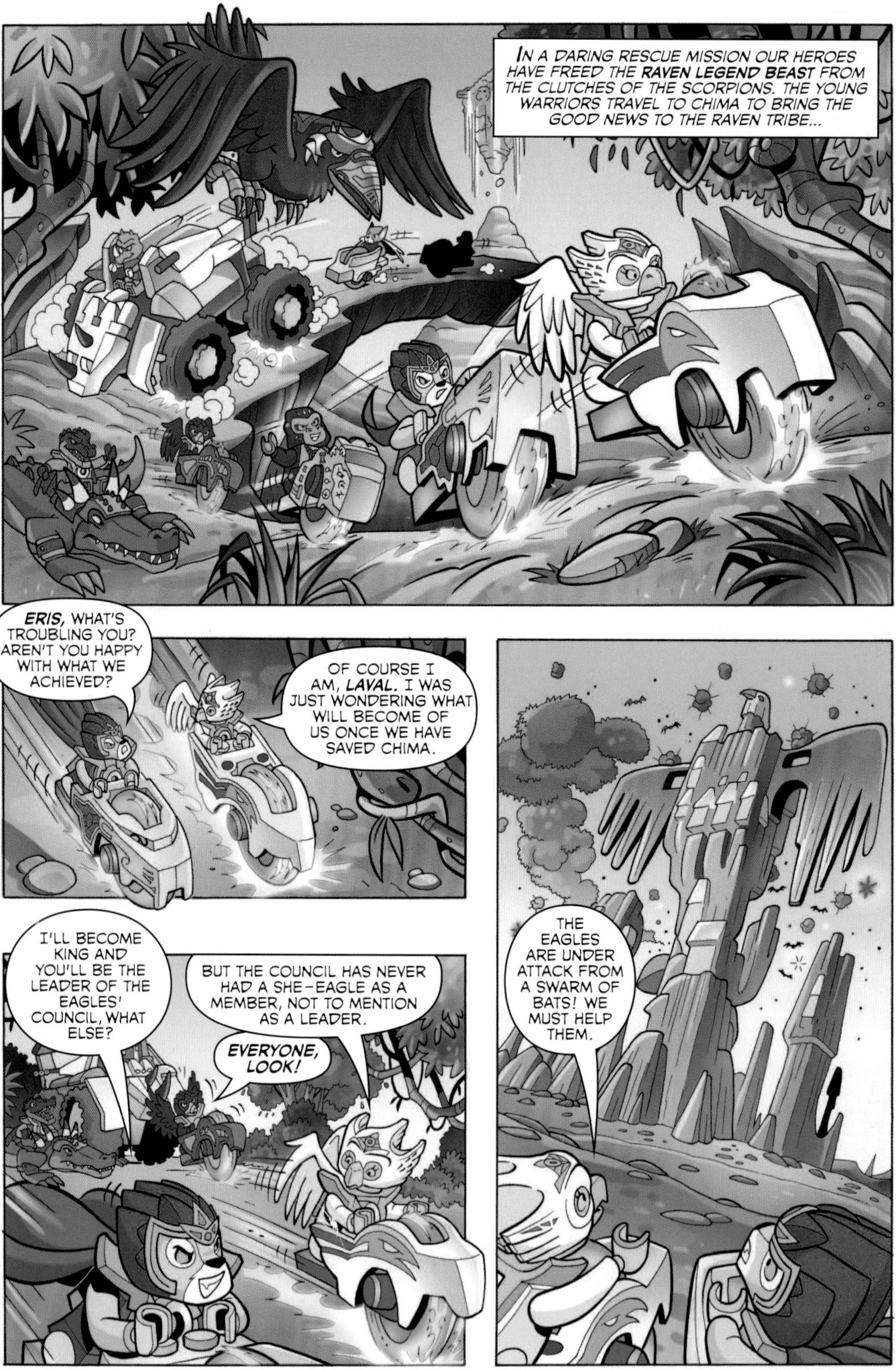
IN A DARING RESCUE MISSION OUR HEROES HAVE FREED THE **RAVEN LEGEND BEAST** FROM THE CLUTCHES OF THE SCORPIONS. THE YOUNG WARRIORS TRAVEL TO CHIMA TO BRING THE GOOD NEWS TO THE RAVEN TRIBE...
ERIS, WHAT'S TROUBLING YOU? AREN'T YOU HAPPY WITH WHAT WE ACHIEVED?
OF COURSE I AM, **LAVAL.** I WAS JUST WONDERING WHAT WILL BECOME OF US ONCE WE HAVE SAVED CHIMA.
I'LL BECOME KING AND YOU'LL BE THE LEADER OF THE EAGLES' COUNCIL, WHAT ELSE?
BUT THE COUNCIL HAS NEVER HAD A SHE-EAGLE AS A MEMBER, NOT TO MENTION AS A LEADER.
EVERYONE, LOOK!
THE EAGLES ARE UNDER ATTACK FROM A SWARM OF BATS! WE MUST HELP THEM.

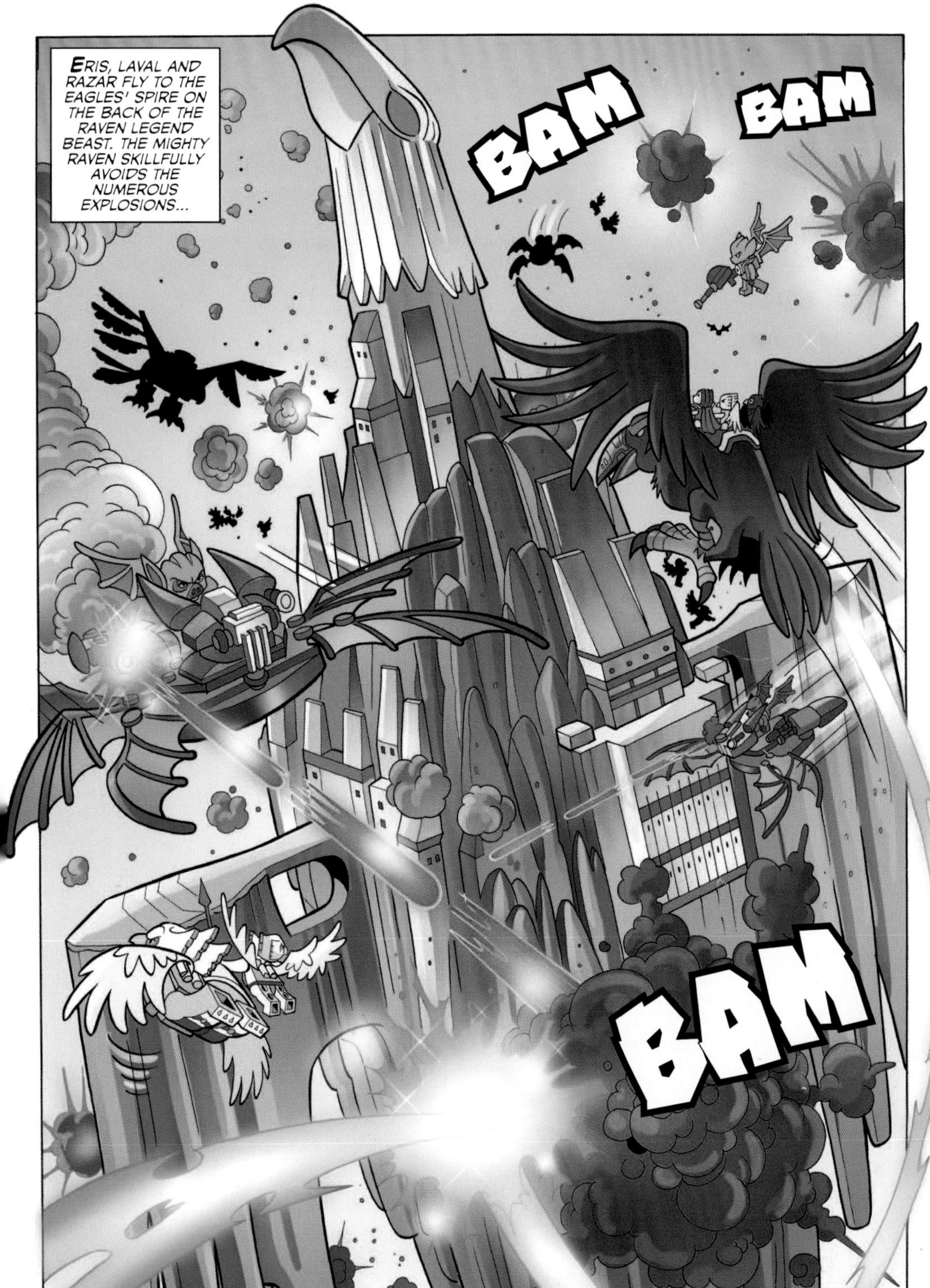
ERIS, LAVAL AND RAZAR FLY TO THE EAGLES' SPIRE ON THE BACK OF THE RAVEN LEGEND BEAST. THE MIGHTY RAVEN SKILLFULLY AVOIDS THE NUMEROUS EXPLOSIONS...
BAM
BAM
BAM

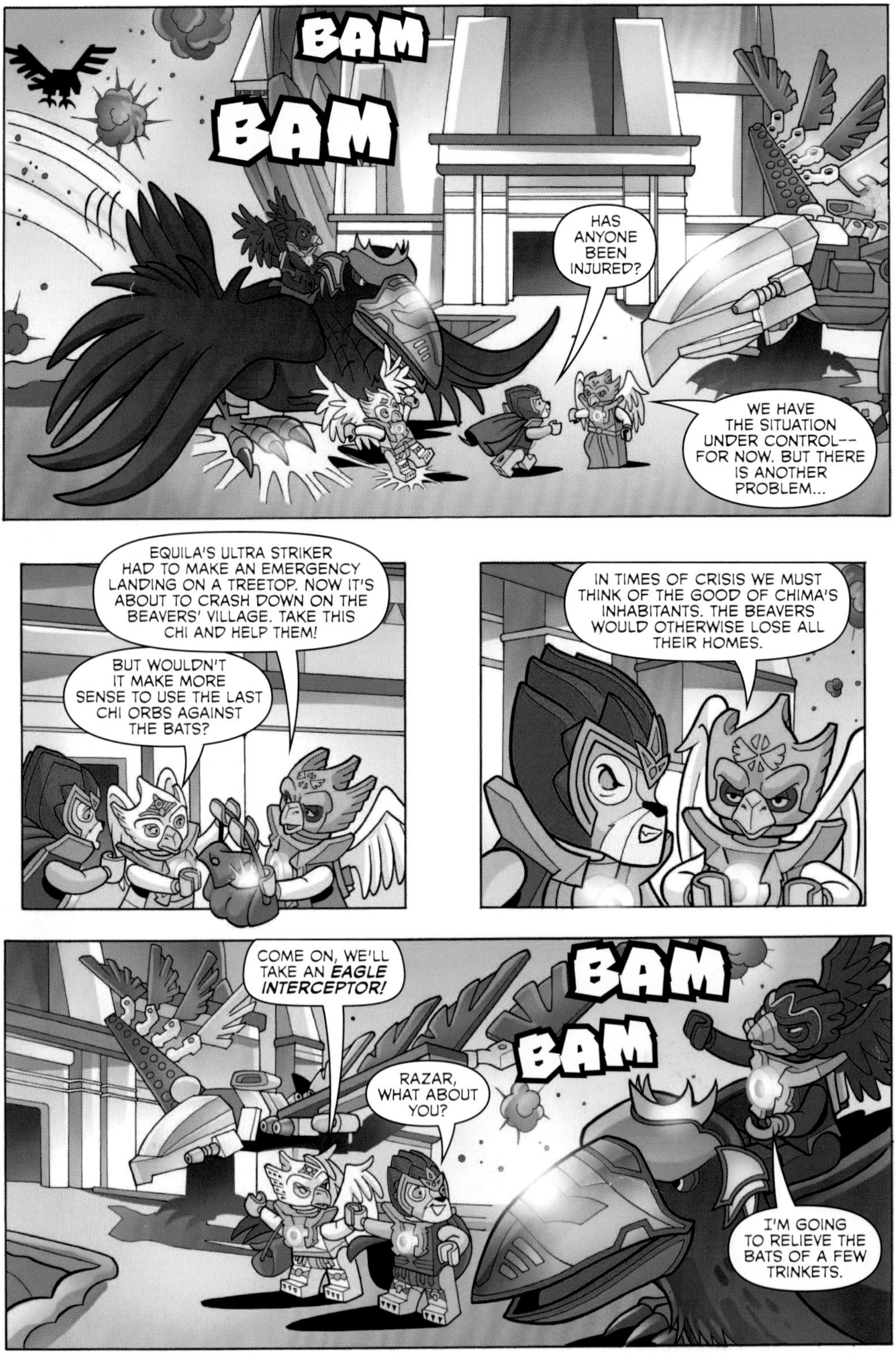
BAM
BAM
HAS ANYONE BEEN INJURED?
WE HAVE THE SITUATION UNDER CONTROL-- FOR NOW. BUT THERE IS ANOTHER PROBLEM...
EQUILA'S ULTRA STRIKER HAD TO MAKE AN EMERGENCY LANDING ON A TREETOP. NOW IT'S ABOUT TO CRASH DOWN ON THE BEAVERS' VILLAGE. TAKE THIS CHI AND HELP THEM!
BUT WOULDN'T IT MAKE MORE SENSE TO USE THE LAST CHI ORBS AGAINST THE BATS?
IN TIMES OF CRISIS WE MUST THINK OF THE GOOD OF CHIMA'S INHABITANTS. THE BEAVERS WOULD OTHERWISE LOSE ALL THEIR HOMES.
COME ON, WE'LL TAKE AN *EAGLE INTERCEPTOR!*
BAM
BAM
RAZAR, WHAT ABOUT YOU?
I'M GOING TO RELIEVE THE BATS OF A FEW TRINKETS.

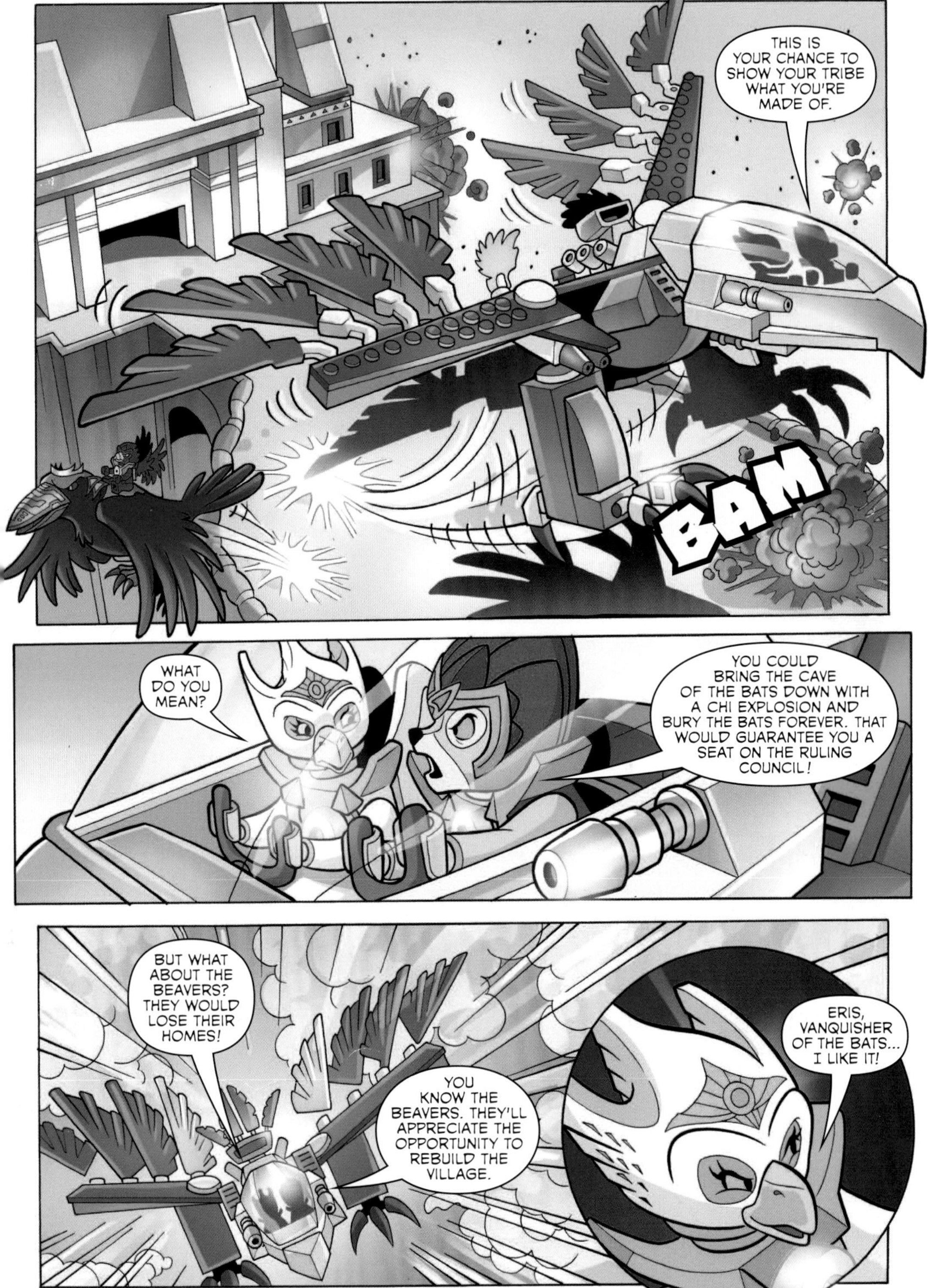
THIS IS YOUR CHANCE TO SHOW YOUR TRIBE WHAT YOU'RE MADE OF.
BAM
WHAT DO YOU MEAN?
YOU COULD BRING THE CAVE OF THE BATS DOWN WITH A CHI EXPLOSION AND BURY THE BATS FOREVER. THAT WOULD GUARANTEE YOU A SEAT ON THE RULING COUNCIL!
BUT WHAT ABOUT THE BEAVERS? THEY WOULD LOSE THEIR HOMES!
YOU KNOW THE BEAVERS. THEY'LL APPRECIATE THE OPPORTUNITY TO REBUILD THE VILLAGE.
ERIS, VANQUISHER OF THE BATS... I LIKE IT!

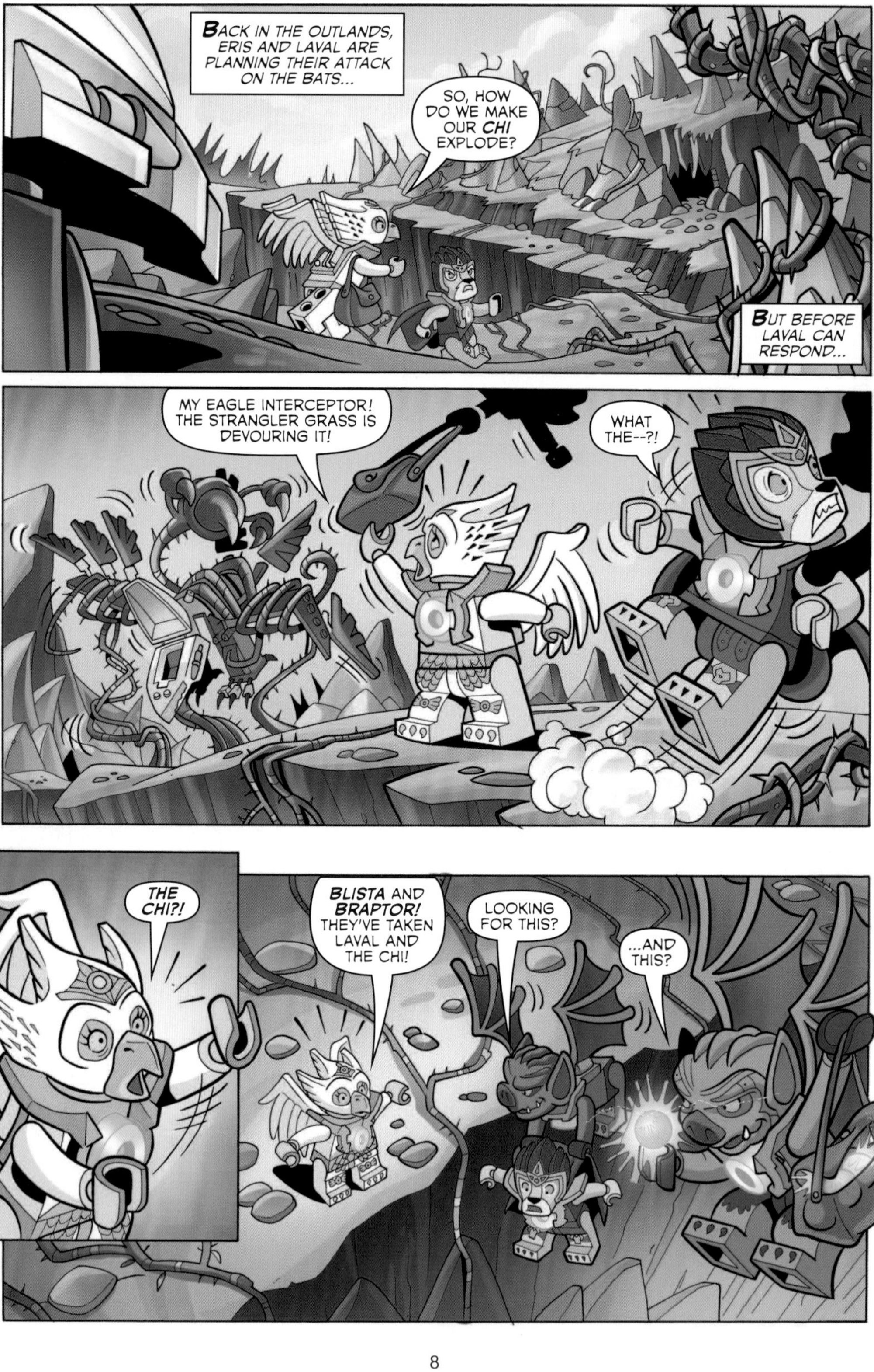
BACK IN THE OUTLANDS, ERIS AND LAVAL ARE PLANNING THEIR ATTACK ON THE BATS...
SO, HOW DO WE MAKE OUR CHI EXPLODE?
BUT BEFORE LAVAL CAN RESPOND...
MY EAGLE INTERCEPTOR! THE STRANGLER GRASS IS DEVOURING IT!
WHAT THE--?!
THE CHI?!
BLISTA AND BRAPTOR! THEY'VE TAKEN LAVAL AND THE CHI!
LOOKING FOR THIS?
...AND THIS?

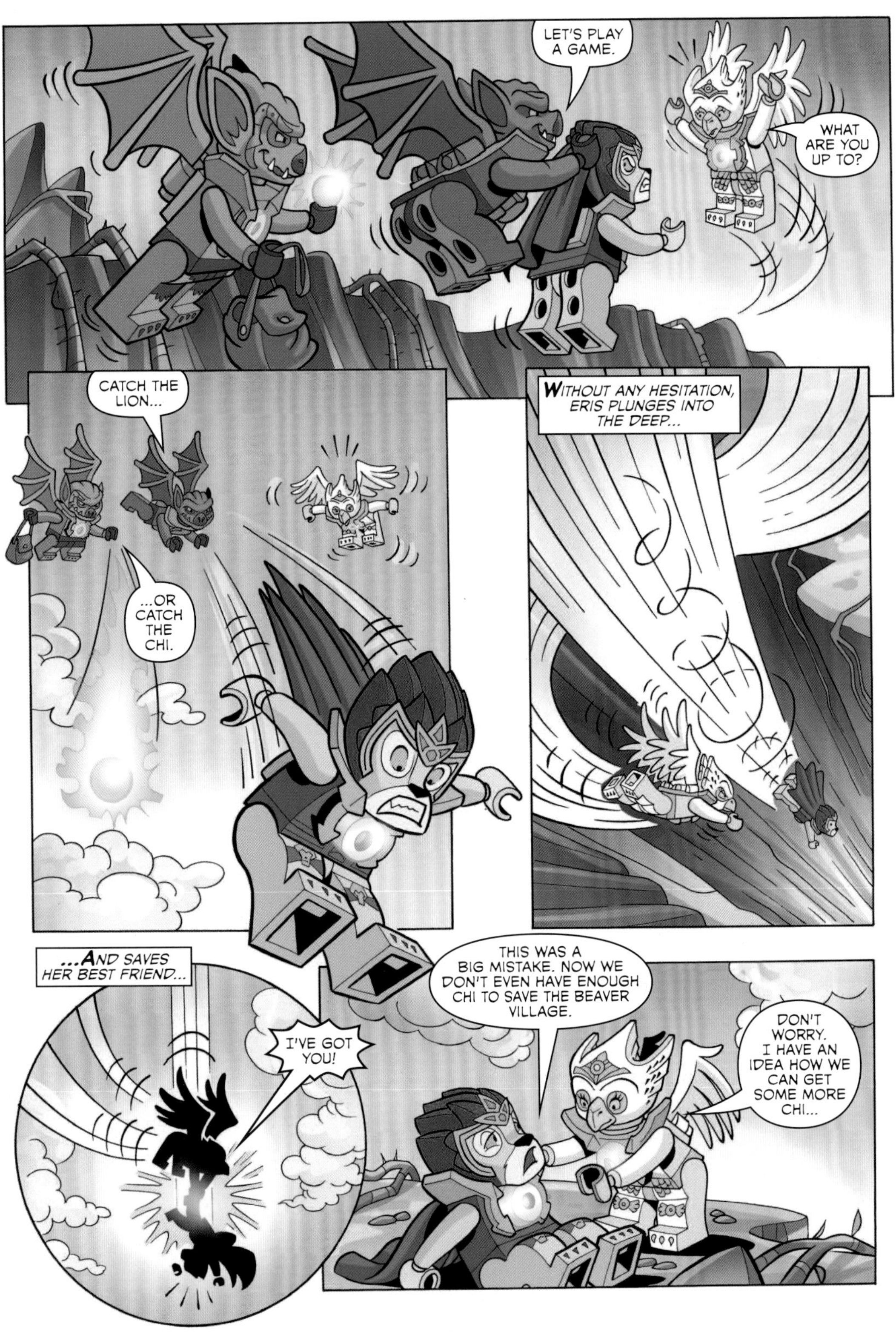
LET'S PLAY A GAME.
WHAT ARE YOU UP TO?
CATCH THE LION...
...OR CATCH THE CHI.
WITHOUT ANY HESITATION, ERIS PLUNGES INTO THE DEEP...
...AND SAVES HER BEST FRIEND...
I'VE GOT YOU!
THIS WAS A BIG MISTAKE. NOW WE DON'T EVEN HAVE ENOUGH CHI TO SAVE THE BEAVER VILLAGE.
DON'T WORRY. I HAVE AN IDEA HOW WE CAN GET SOME MORE CHI...

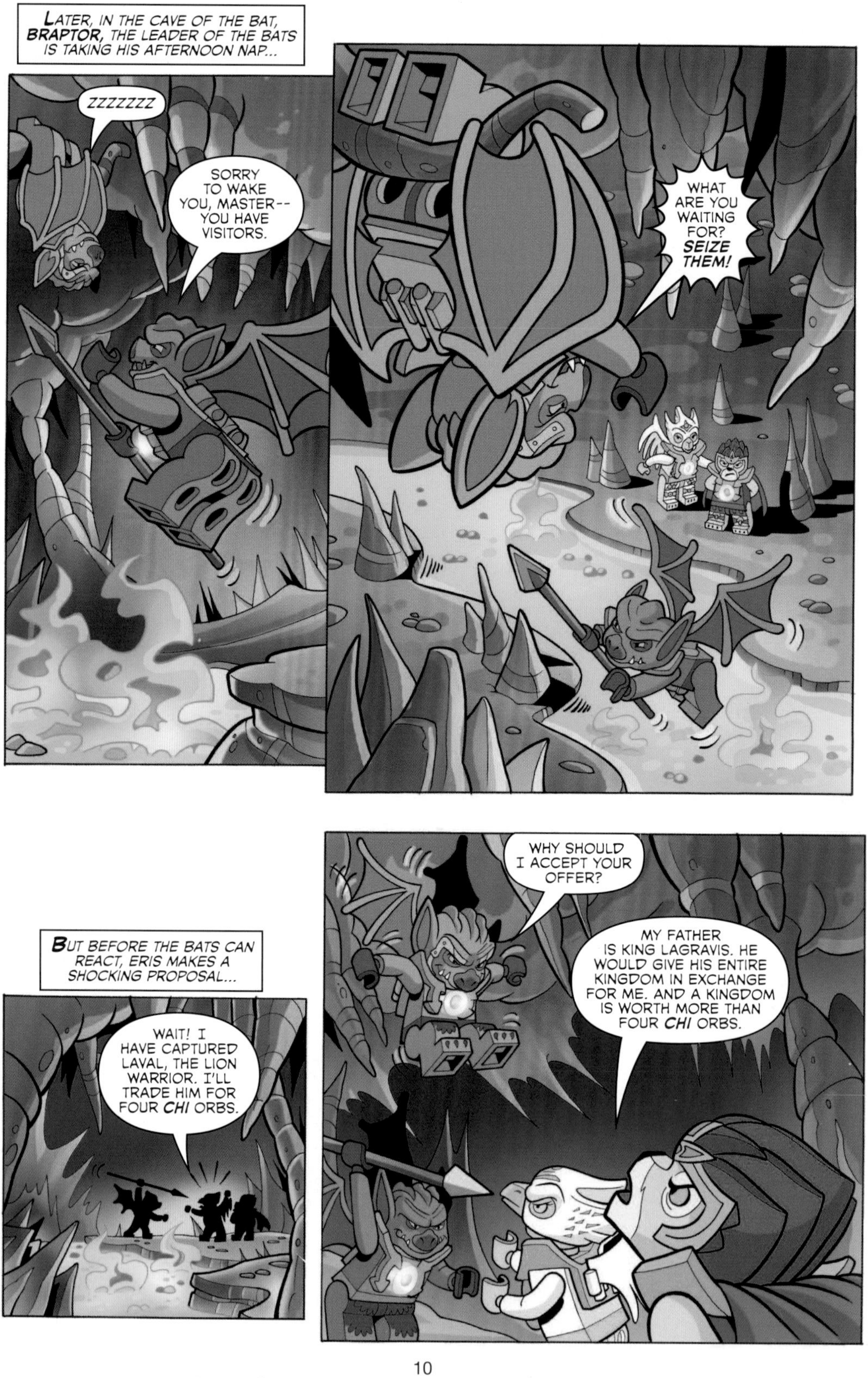
LATER, IN THE CAVE OF THE BAT, BRAPTOR, THE LEADER OF THE BATS IS TAKING HIS AFTERNOON NAP...
ZZZZZZZ
SORRY TO WAKE YOU, MASTER-- YOU HAVE VISITORS.
WHAT ARE YOU WAITING FOR? SEIZE THEM!
BUT BEFORE THE BATS CAN REACT, ERIS MAKES A SHOCKING PROPOSAL...
WAIT! I HAVE CAPTURED LAVAL, THE LION WARRIOR. I'LL TRADE HIM FOR FOUR CHI ORBS.
WHY SHOULD I ACCEPT YOUR OFFER?
MY FATHER IS KING LAGRAVIS. HE WOULD GIVE HIS ENTIRE KINGDOM IN EXCHANGE FOR ME. AND A KINGDOM IS WORTH MORE THAN FOUR CHI ORBS.

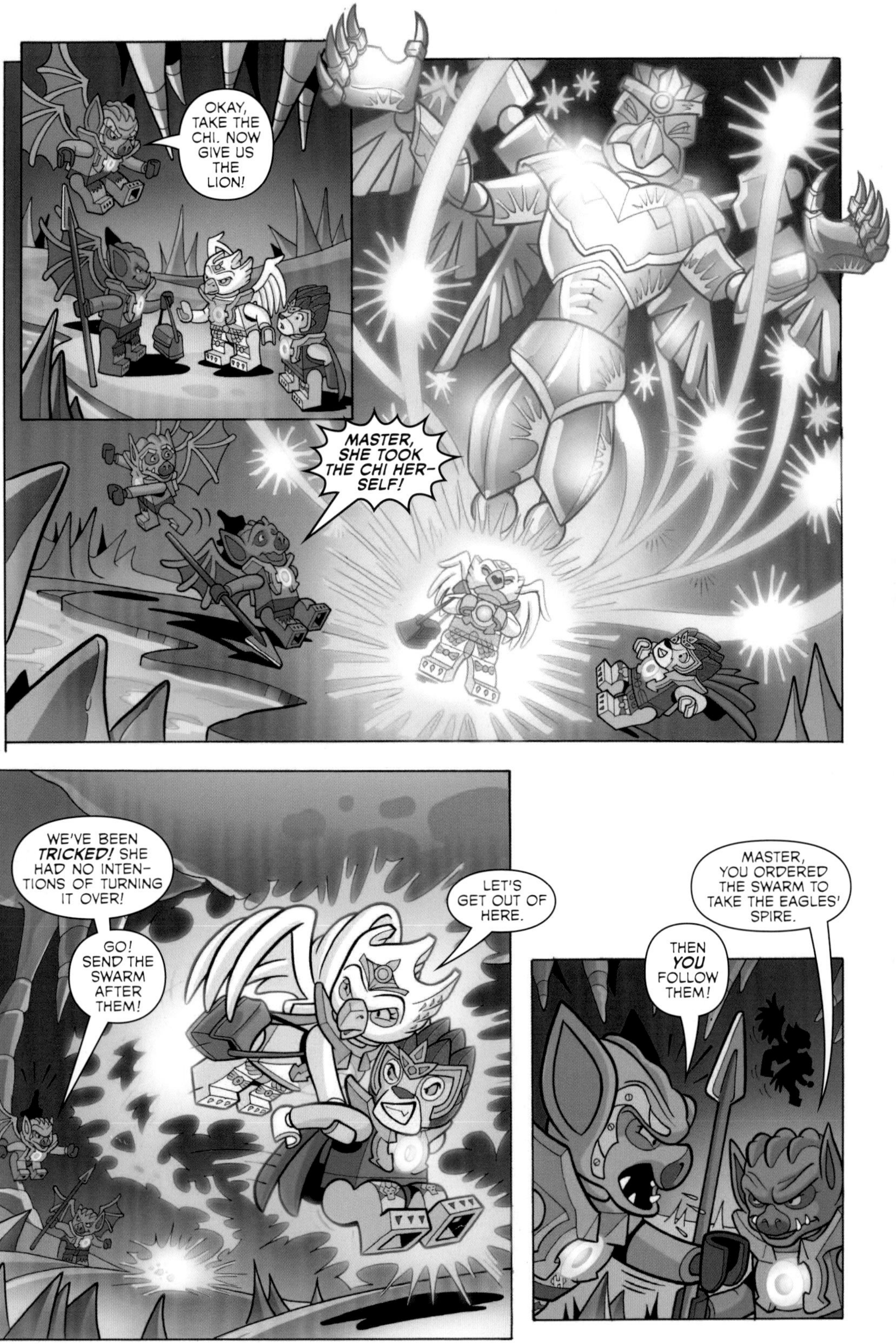
OKAY, TAKE THE CHI. NOW GIVE US THE LION!
MASTER, SHE TOOK THE CHI HER-SELF!
WE'VE BEEN **TRICKED!** SHE HAD NO INTEN-TIONS OF TURNING IT OVER!
GO! SEND THE SWARM AFTER THEM!
LET'S GET OUT OF HERE.
MASTER, YOU ORDERED THE SWARM TO TAKE THE EAGLES' SPIRE.
THEN **YOU** FOLLOW THEM!

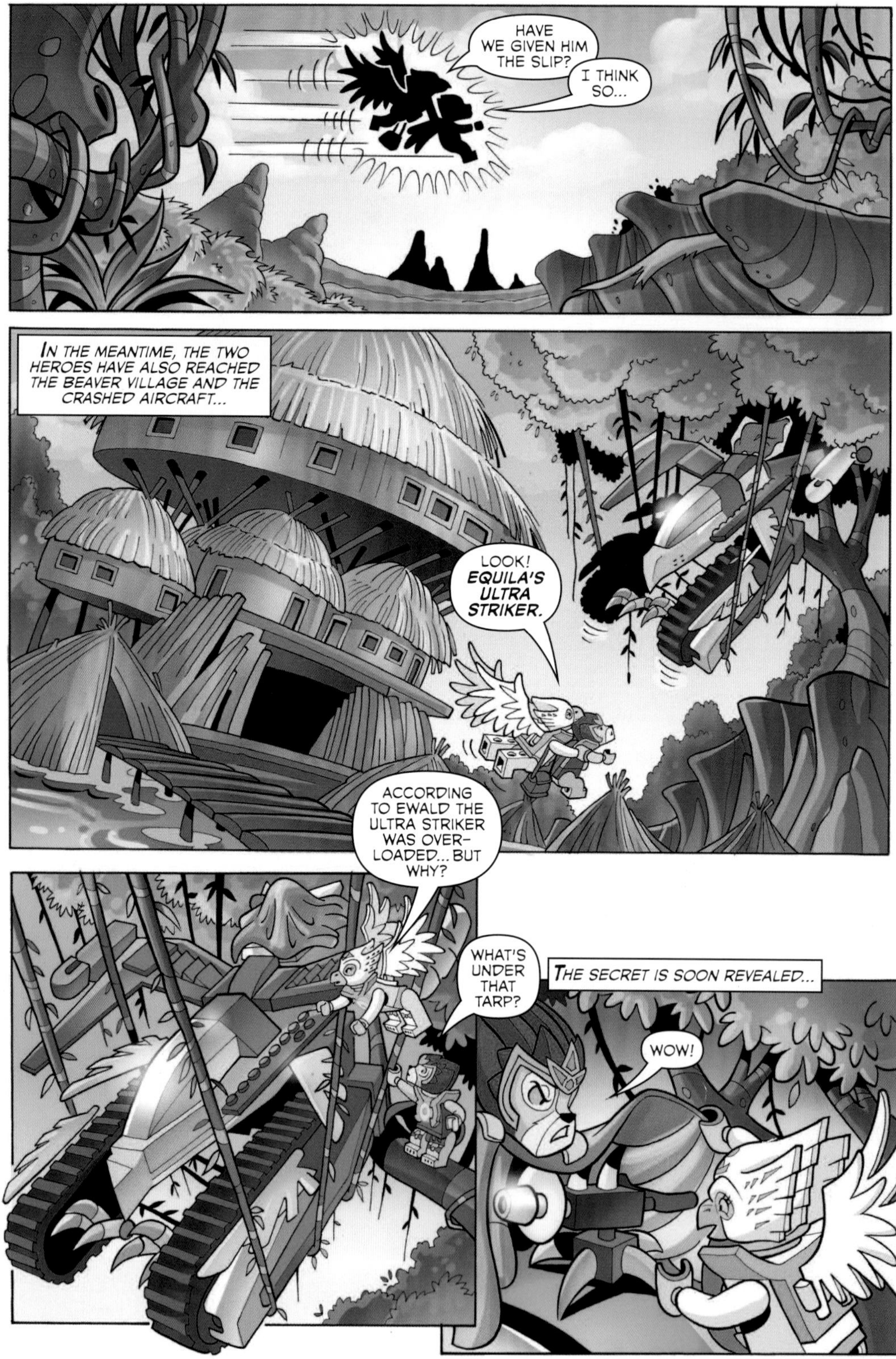

HAVE WE GIVEN HIM THE SLIP?
I THINK SO...
IN THE MEANTIME, THE TWO HEROES HAVE ALSO REACHED THE BEAVER VILLAGE AND THE CRASHED AIRCRAFT...
LOOK! EQUILA'S ULTRA STRIKER.
ACCORDING TO EWALD THE ULTRA STRIKER WAS OVER-LOADED... BUT WHY?
WHAT'S UNDER THAT TARP?
THE SECRET IS SOON REVEALED...
WOW!

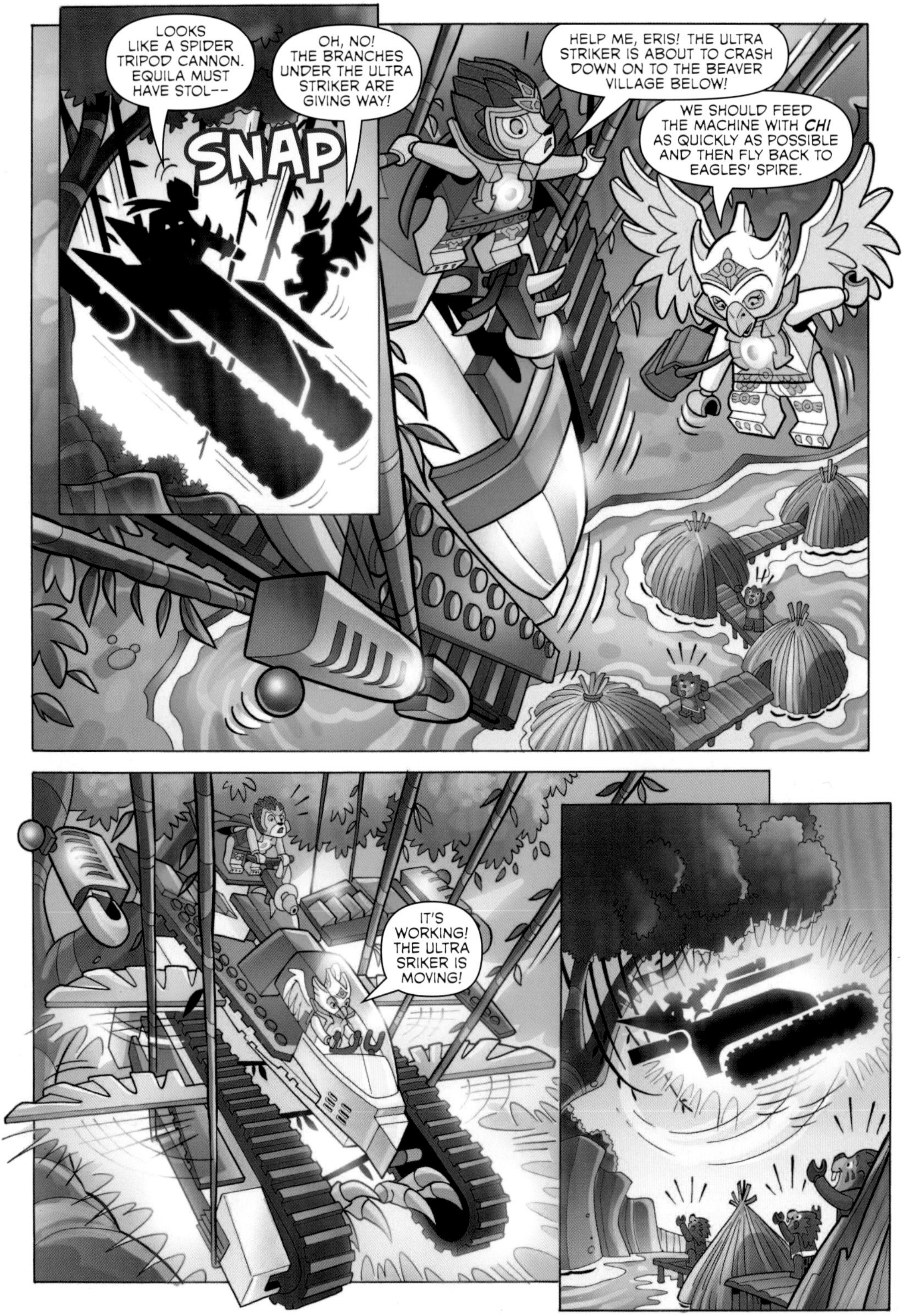
LOOKS LIKE A SPIDER TRIPOD CANNON. EQUILA MUST HAVE STOL--
SNAP
OH, NO! THE BRANCHES UNDER THE ULTRA STRIKER ARE GIVING WAY!
HELP ME, ERIS! THE ULTRA STRIKER IS ABOUT TO CRASH DOWN ON TO THE BEAVER VILLAGE BELOW!
WE SHOULD FEED THE MACHINE WITH CHI AS QUICKLY AS POSSIBLE AND THEN FLY BACK TO EAGLES' SPIRE.
IT'S WORKING! THE ULTRA SRIKER IS MOVING!

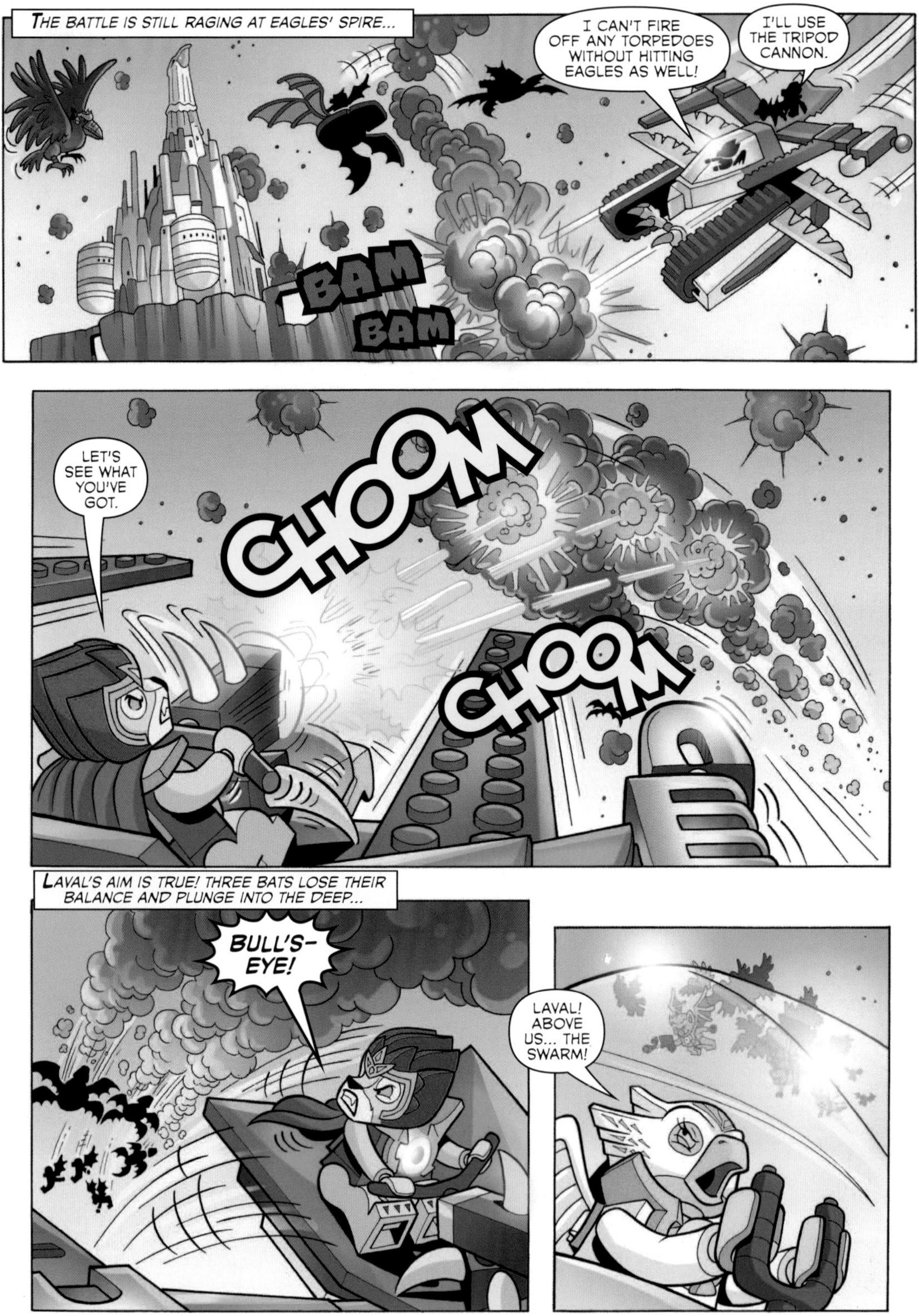
THE BATTLE IS STILL RAGING AT EAGLES' SPIRE...
I CAN'T FIRE OFF ANY TORPEDOES WITHOUT HITTING EAGLES AS WELL!
I'LL USE THE TRIPOD CANNON.
BAM
BAM
LET'S SEE WHAT YOU'VE GOT.
CHOOM
CHOOM
LAVAL'S AIM IS TRUE! THREE BATS LOSE THEIR BALANCE AND PLUNGE INTO THE DEEP...
BULL'S-EYE!
LAVAL! ABOVE US... THE SWARM!

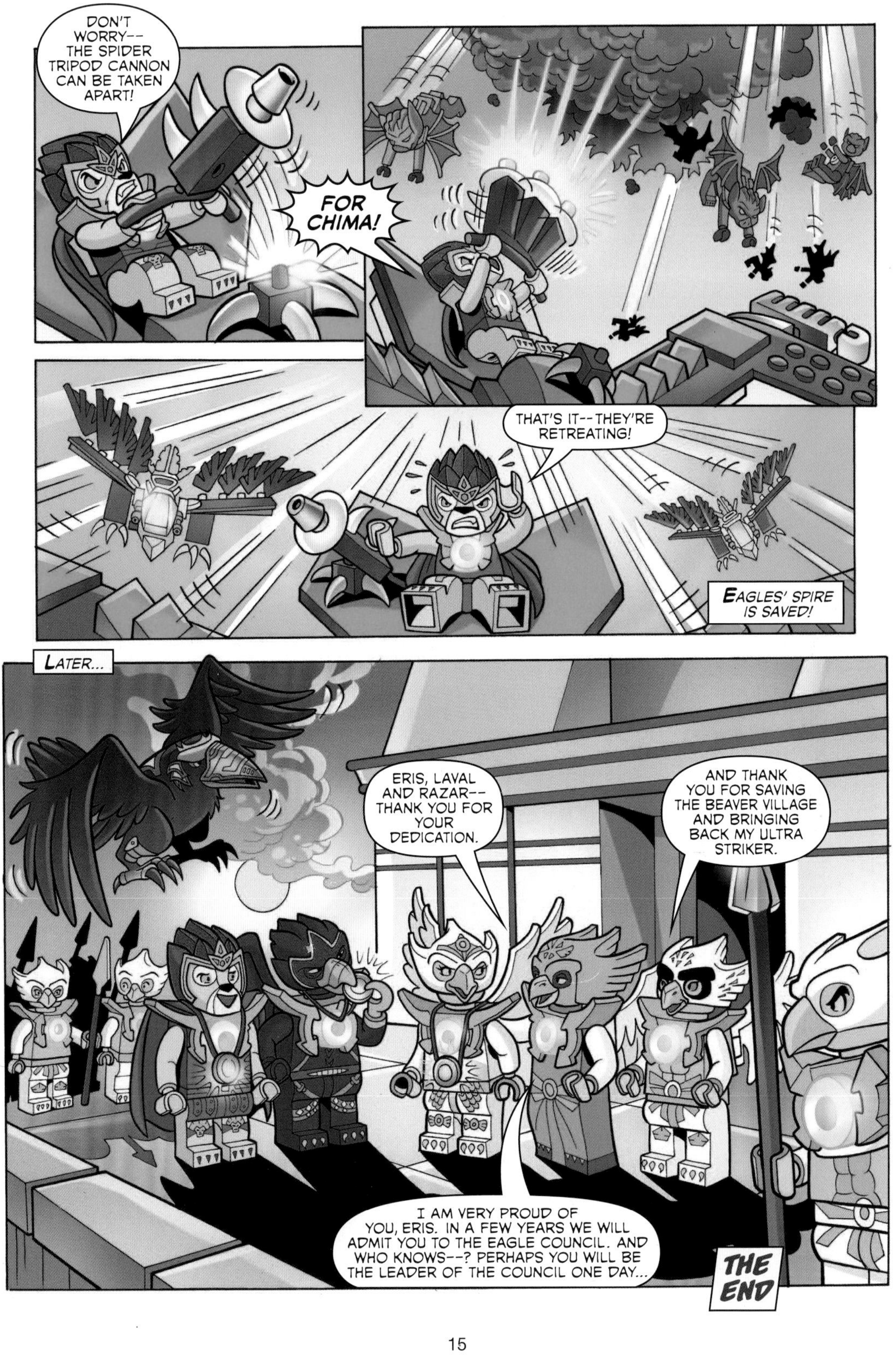
DON'T WORRY-- THE SPIDER TRIPOD CANNON CAN BE TAKEN APART!
FOR CHIMA!
THAT'S IT--THEY'RE RETREATING!
EAGLES' SPIRE IS SAVED!
LATER...
ERIS, LAVAL AND RAZAR-- THANK YOU FOR YOUR DEDICATION.
AND THANK YOU FOR SAVING THE BEAVER VILLAGE AND BRINGING BACK MY ULTRA STRIKER.
I AM VERY PROUD OF YOU, ERIS. IN A FEW YEARS WE WILL ADMIT YOU TO THE EAGLE COUNCIL. AND WHO KNOWS--? PERHAPS YOU WILL BE THE LEADER OF THE COUNCIL ONE DAY...
THE END

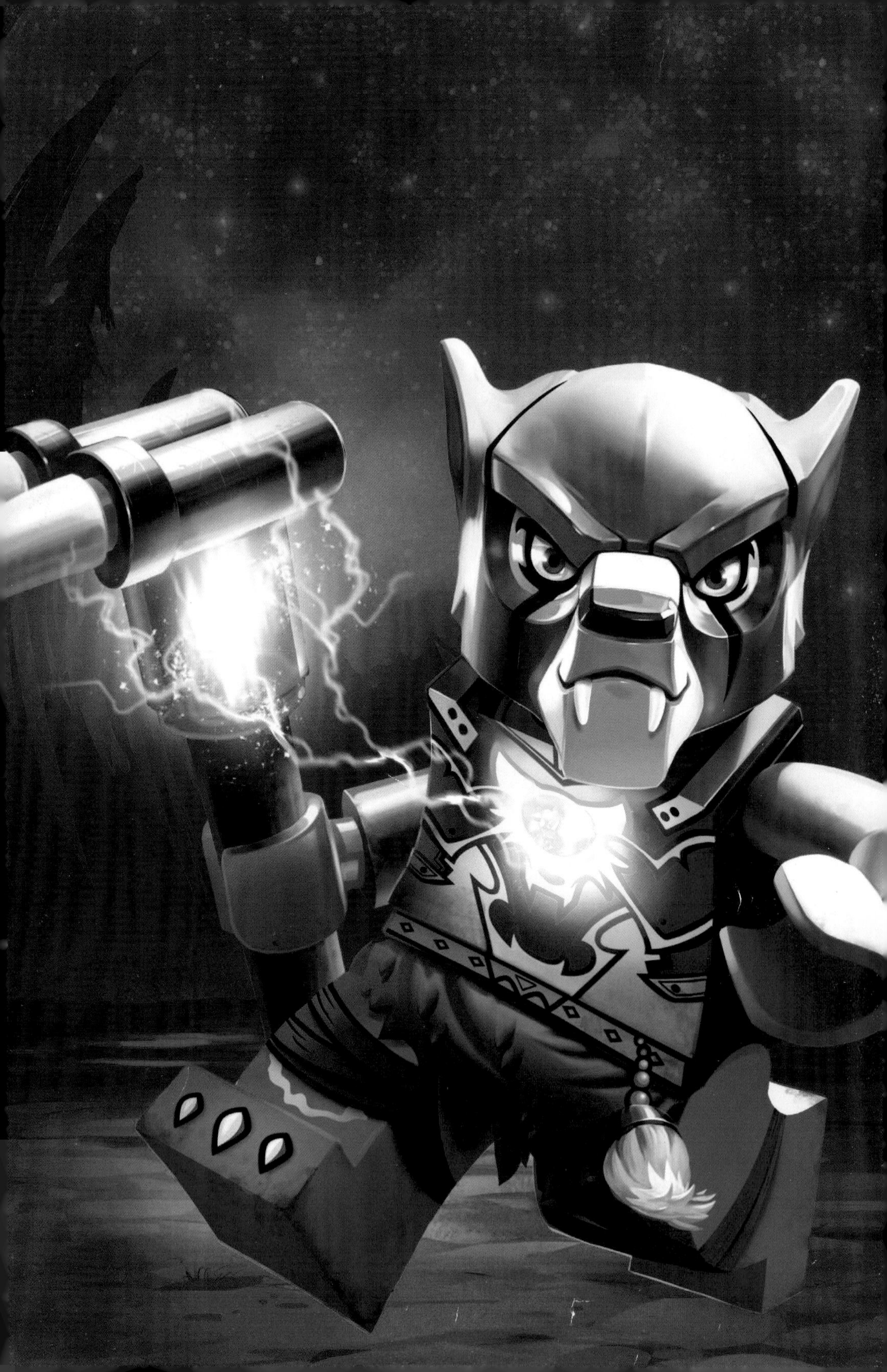

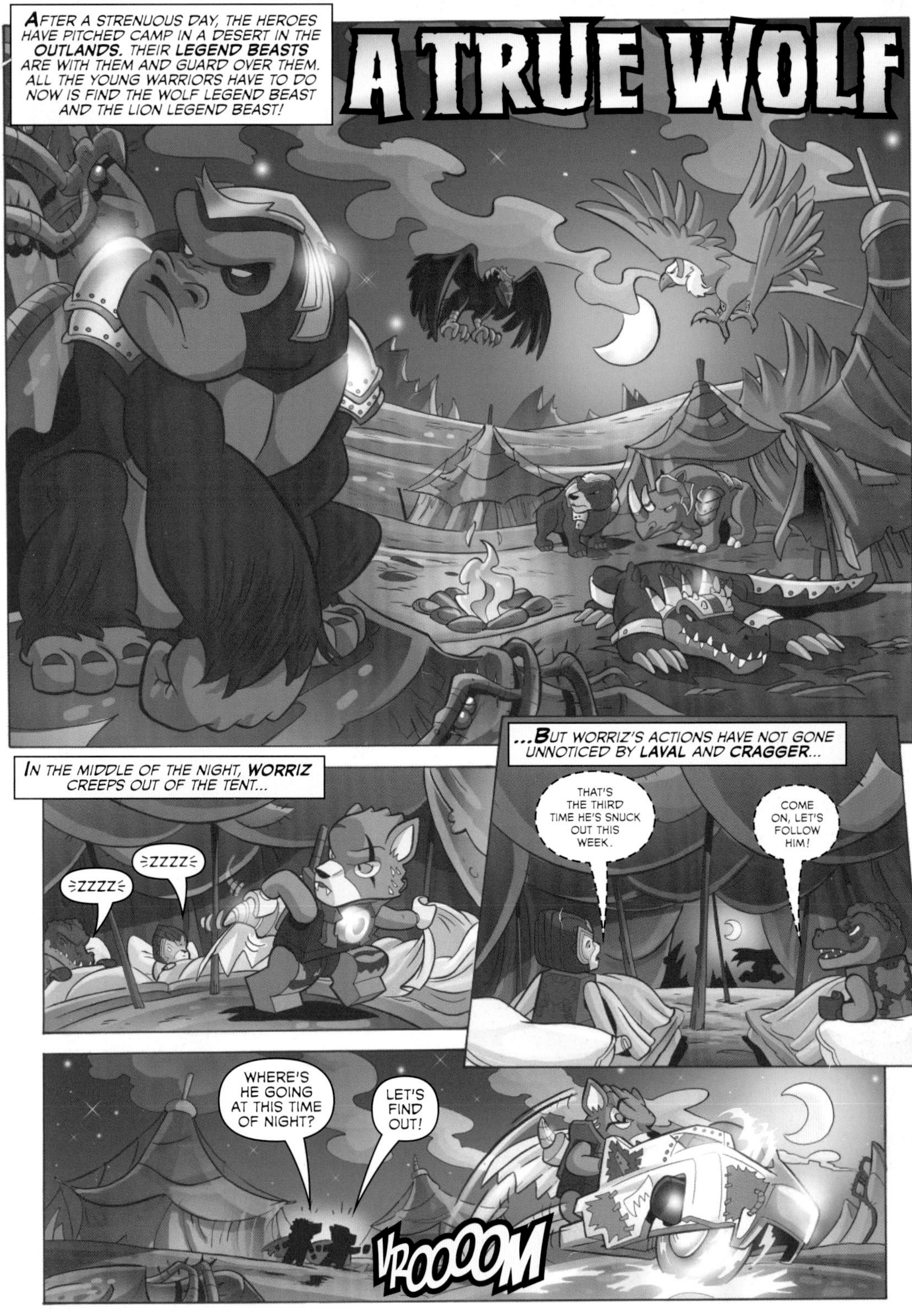
AFTER A STRENUOUS DAY, THE HEROES HAVE PITCHED CAMP IN A DESERT IN THE OUTLANDS. THEIR LEGEND BEASTS ARE WITH THEM AND GUARD OVER THEM. ALL THE YOUNG WARRIORS HAVE TO DO NOW IS FIND THE WOLF LEGEND BEAST AND THE LION LEGEND BEAST!
A TRUE WOLF
IN THE MIDDLE OF THE NIGHT, WORRIZ CREEPS OUT OF THE TENT...
ZZZZ
ZZZZ
...BUT WORRIZ'S ACTIONS HAVE NOT GONE UNNOTICED BY LAVAL AND CRAGGER...
THAT'S THE THIRD TIME HE'S SNUCK OUT THIS WEEK.
COME ON, LET'S FOLLOW HIM!
WHERE'S HE GOING AT THIS TIME OF NIGHT?
LET'S FIND OUT!
VROOOOM

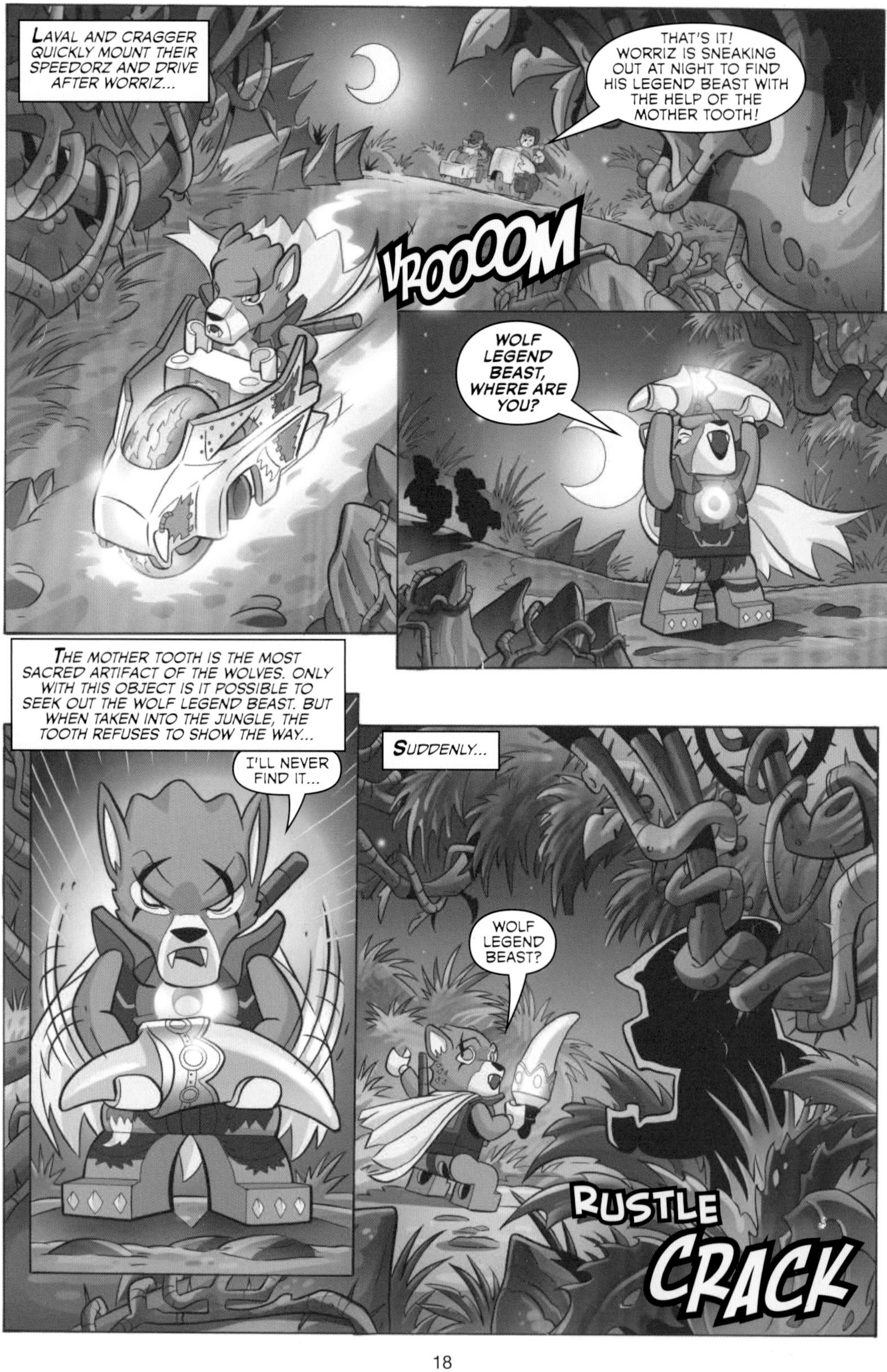
LAVAL AND CRAGGER QUICKLY MOUNT THEIR SPEEDORZ AND DRIVE AFTER WORRIZ...
THAT'S IT! WORRIZ IS SNEAKING OUT AT NIGHT TO FIND HIS LEGEND BEAST WITH THE HELP OF THE MOTHER TOOTH!
VROOOOM
WOLF LEGEND BEAST, WHERE ARE YOU?
THE MOTHER TOOTH IS THE MOST SACRED ARTIFACT OF THE WOLVES. ONLY WITH THIS OBJECT IS IT POSSIBLE TO SEEK OUT THE WOLF LEGEND BEAST. BUT WHEN TAKEN INTO THE JUNGLE, THE TOOTH REFUSES TO SHOW THE WAY...
I'LL NEVER FIND IT...
SUDDENLY...
WOLF LEGEND BEAST?
RUSTLE
CRACK

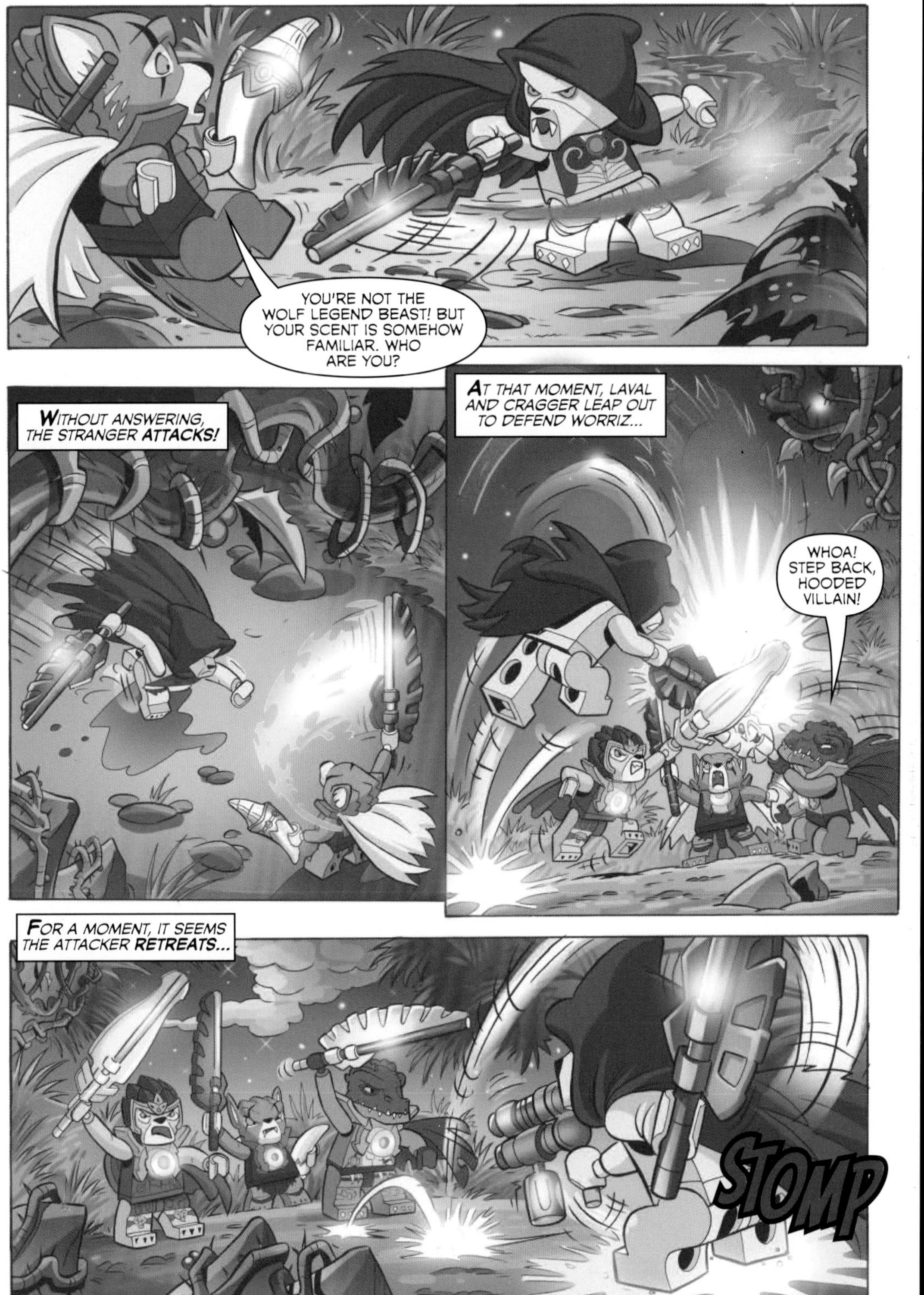
YOU'RE NOT THE WOLF LEGEND BEAST! BUT YOUR SCENT IS SOMEHOW FAMILIAR. WHO ARE YOU?
WITHOUT ANSWERING, THE STRANGER ATTACKS!
AT THAT MOMENT, LAVAL AND CRAGGER LEAP OUT TO DEFEND WORRIZ...
WHOA! STEP BACK, HOODED VILLAIN!
FOR A MOMENT, IT SEEMS THE ATTACKER RETREATS...
STOMP

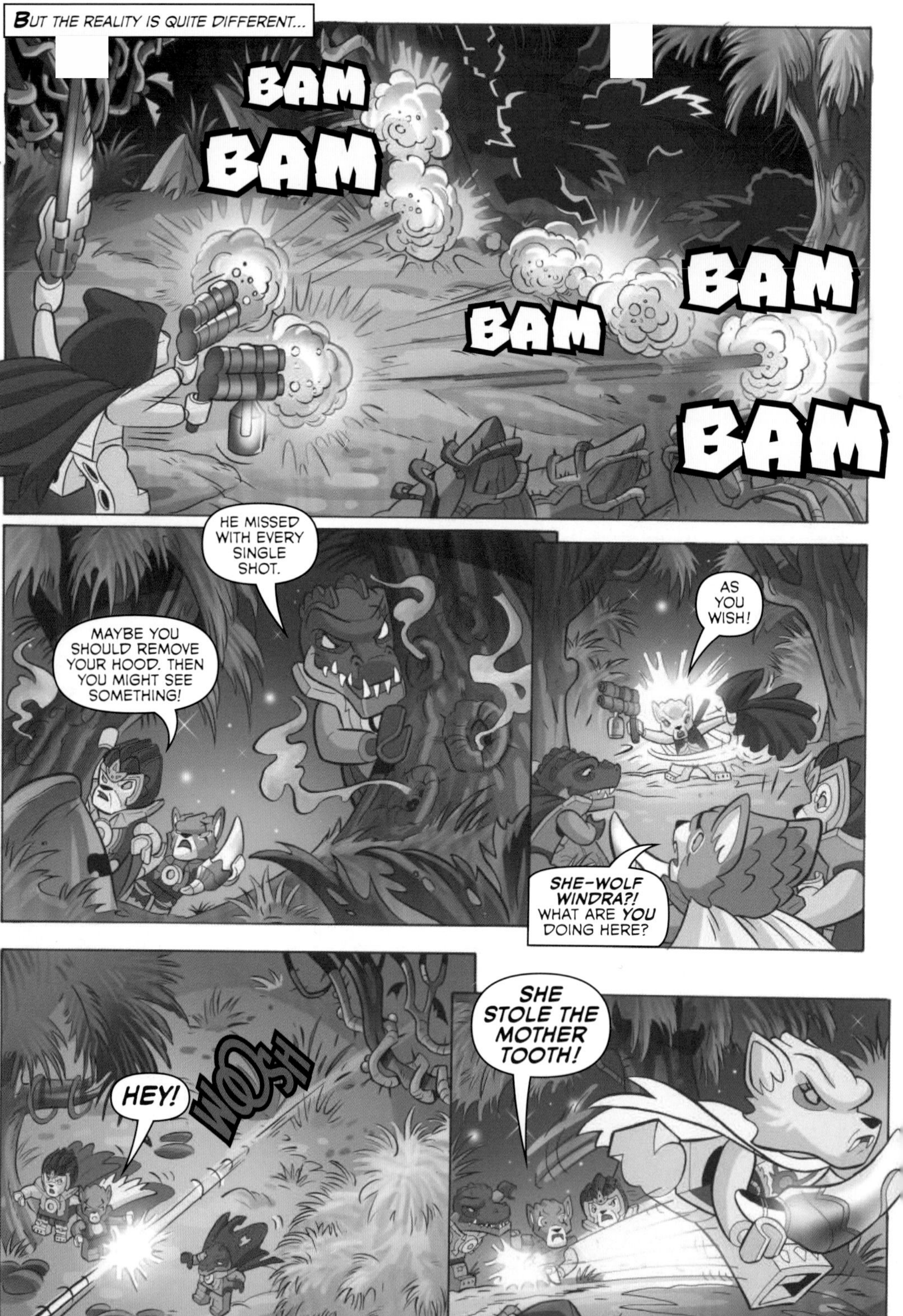
BUT THE REALITY IS QUITE DIFFERENT...
BAM
BAM
BAM
BAM
BAM
HE MISSED WITH EVERY SINGLE SHOT.
MAYBE YOU SHOULD REMOVE YOUR HOOD. THEN YOU MIGHT SEE SOMETHING!
AS YOU WISH!
SHE-WOLF WINDRA?! WHAT ARE YOU DOING HERE?
HEY!
WOOSH
SHE STOLE THE MOTHER TOOTH!

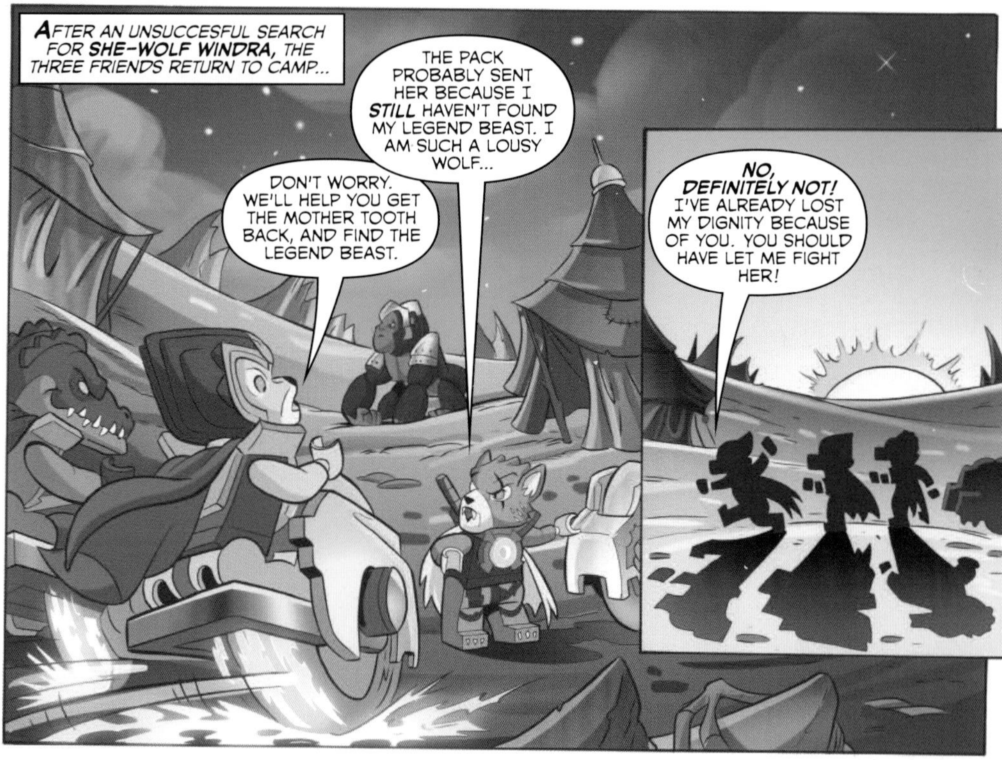
AFTER AN UNSUCCESFUL SEARCH FOR SHE-WOLF WINDRA, THE THREE FRIENDS RETURN TO CAMP...
DON'T WORRY. WE'LL HELP YOU GET THE MOTHER TOOTH BACK, AND FIND THE LEGEND BEAST.
THE PACK PROBABLY SENT HER BECAUSE I STILL HAVEN'T FOUND MY LEGEND BEAST. I AM SUCH A LOUSY WOLF...
NO, DEFINITELY NOT! I'VE ALREADY LOST MY DIGNITY BECAUSE OF YOU. YOU SHOULD HAVE LET ME FIGHT HER!

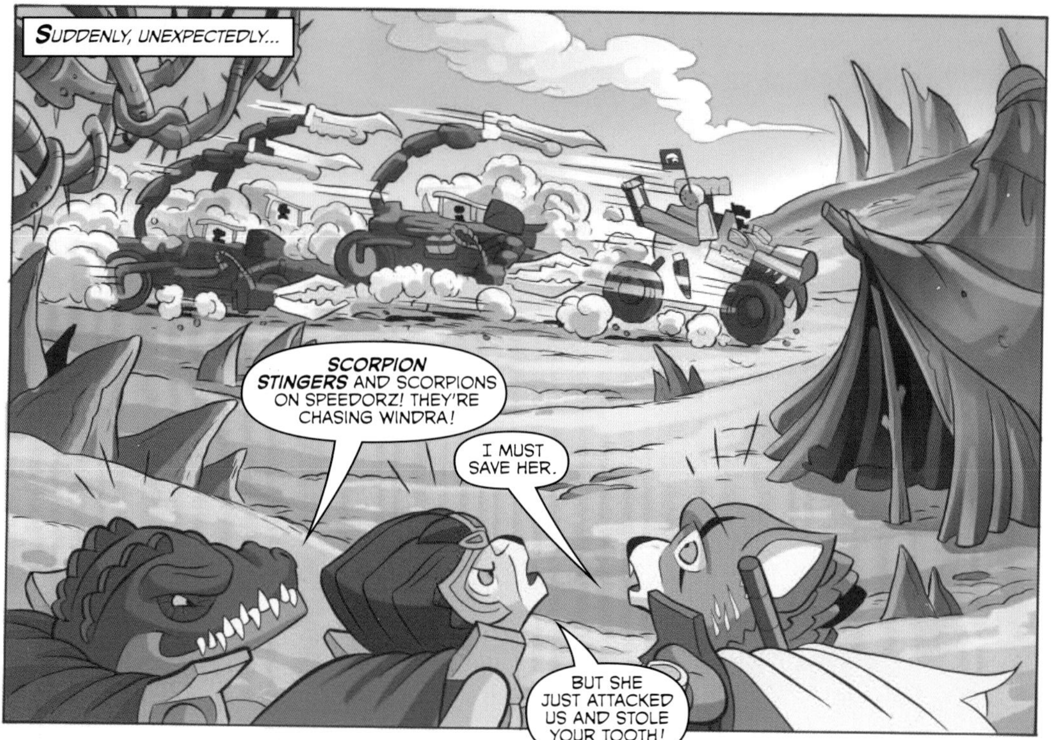
SUDDENLY, UNEXPECTEDLY...
SCORPION STINGERS AND SCORPIONS ON SPEEDORZ! THEY'RE CHASING WINDRA!
I MUST SAVE HER.
BUT SHE JUST ATTACKED US AND STOLE YOUR TOOTH!

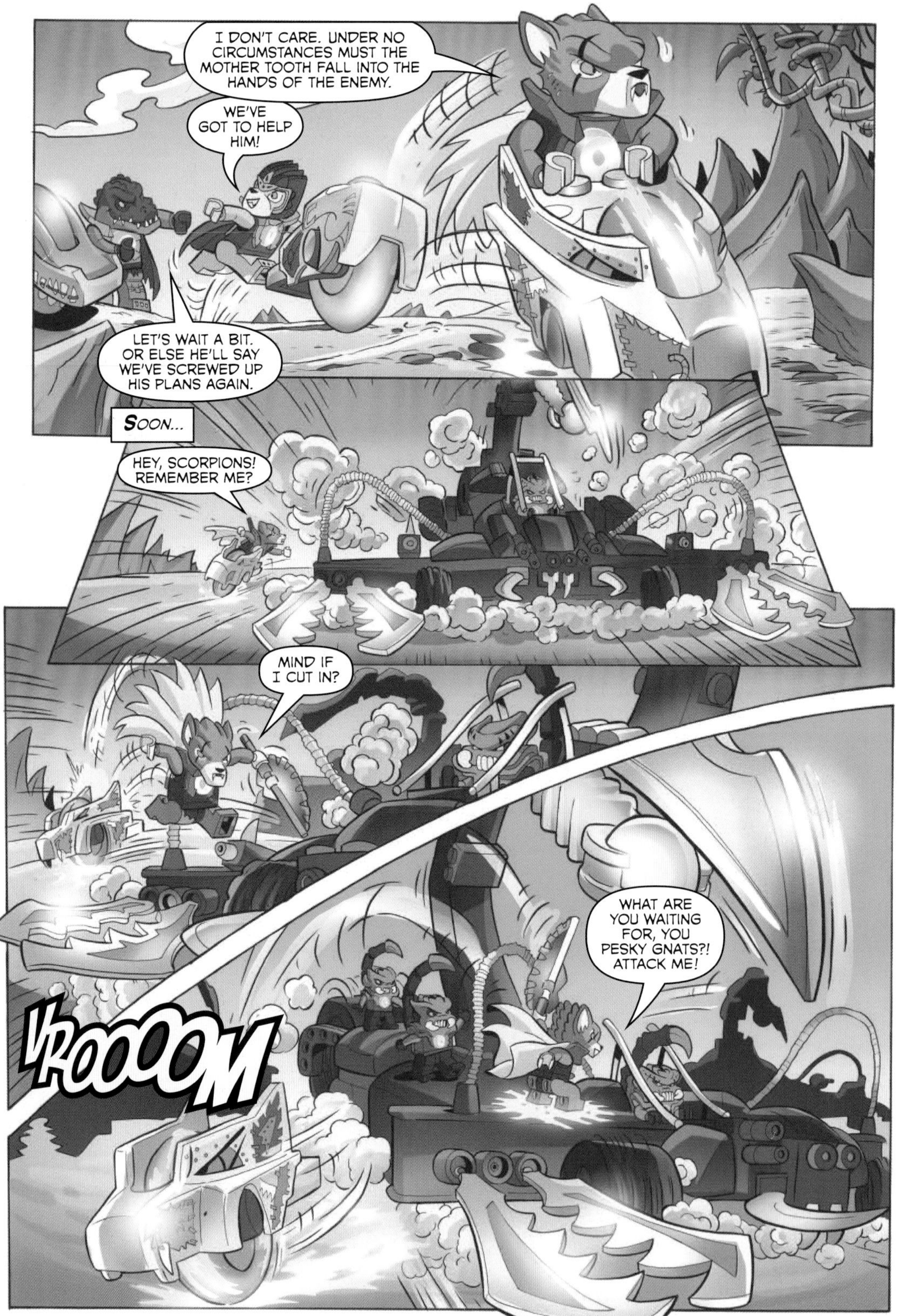
I DON'T CARE. UNDER NO CIRCUMSTANCES MUST THE MOTHER TOOTH FALL INTO THE HANDS OF THE ENEMY.
WE'VE GOT TO HELP HIM!
LET'S WAIT A BIT. OR ELSE HE'LL SAY WE'VE SCREWED UP HIS PLANS AGAIN.
SOON...
HEY, SCORPIONS! REMEMBER ME?
MIND IF I CUT IN?
WHAT ARE YOU WAITING FOR, YOU PESKY GNATS?! ATTACK ME!
VROOOOM

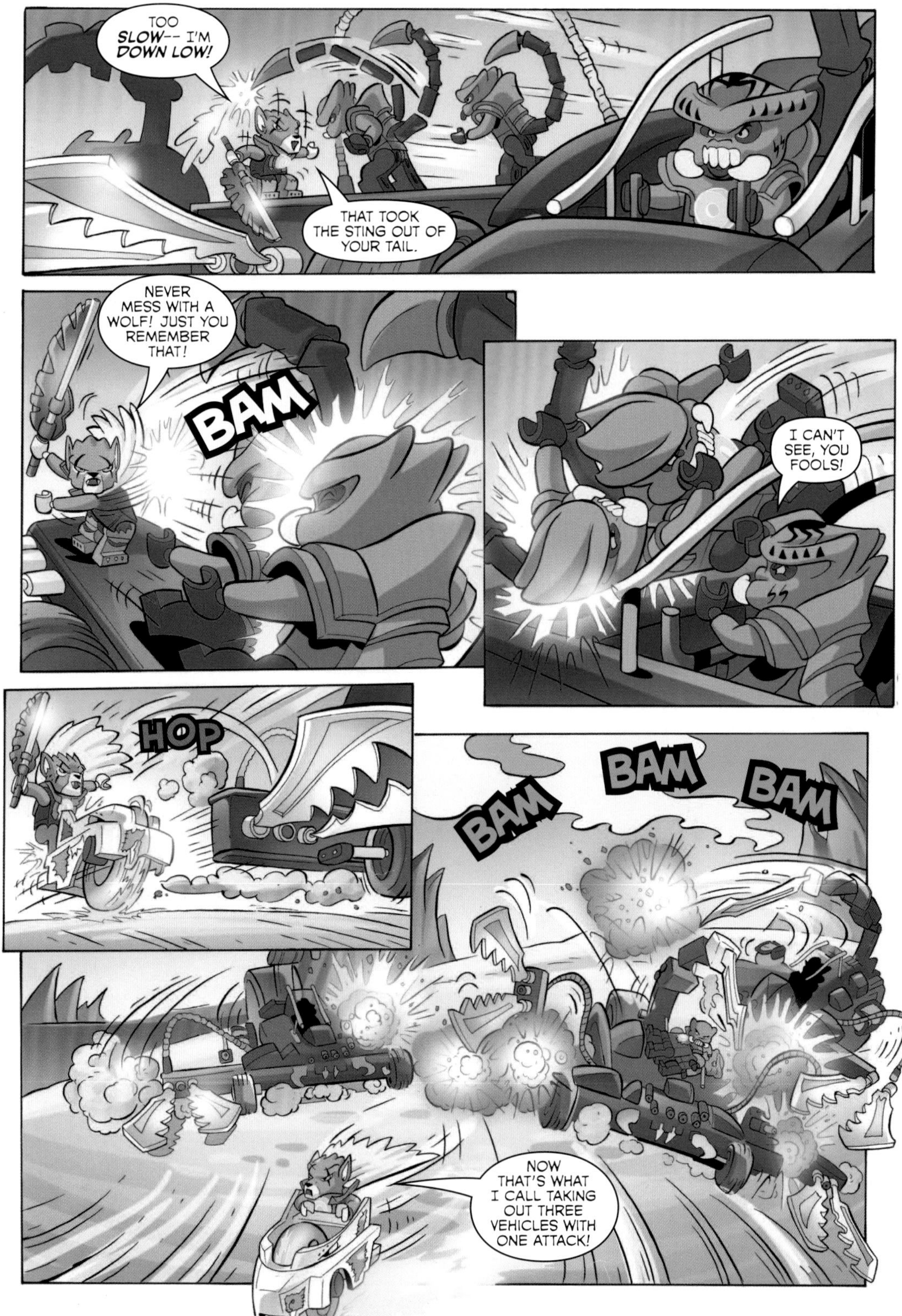
TOO SLOW-- I'M DOWN LOW!
THAT TOOK THE STING OUT OF YOUR TAIL.
NEVER MESS WITH A WOLF! JUST YOU REMEMBER THAT!
BAM
I CAN'T SEE, YOU FOOLS!
HOP
BAM
BAM
BAM
NOW THAT'S WHAT I CALL TAKING OUT THREE VEHICLES WITH ONE ATTACK!

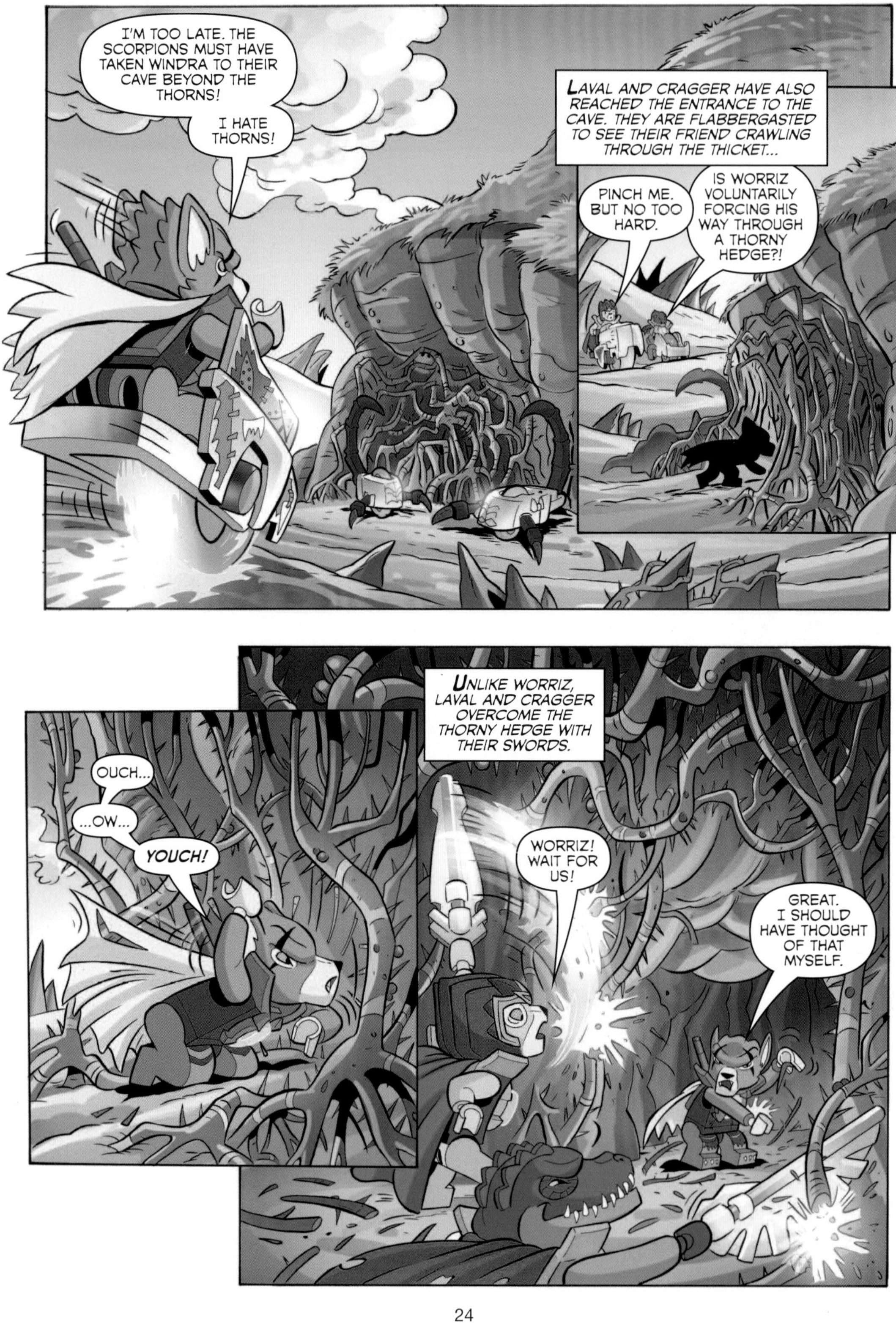
I'M TOO LATE. THE SCORPIONS MUST HAVE TAKEN WINDRA TO THEIR CAVE BEYOND THE THORNS!
I HATE THORNS!
LAVAL AND CRAGGER HAVE ALSO REACHED THE ENTRANCE TO THE CAVE. THEY ARE FLABBERGASTED TO SEE THEIR FRIEND CRAWLING THROUGH THE THICKET...
PINCH ME. BUT NO TOO HARD.
IS WORRIZ VOLUNTARILY FORCING HIS WAY THROUGH A THORNY HEDGE?!
OUCH...
...OW...
YOUCH!
UNLIKE WORRIZ, LAVAL AND CRAGGER OVERCOME THE THORNY HEDGE WITH THEIR SWORDS.
WORRIZ! WAIT FOR US!
GREAT. I SHOULD HAVE THOUGHT OF THAT MYSELF.

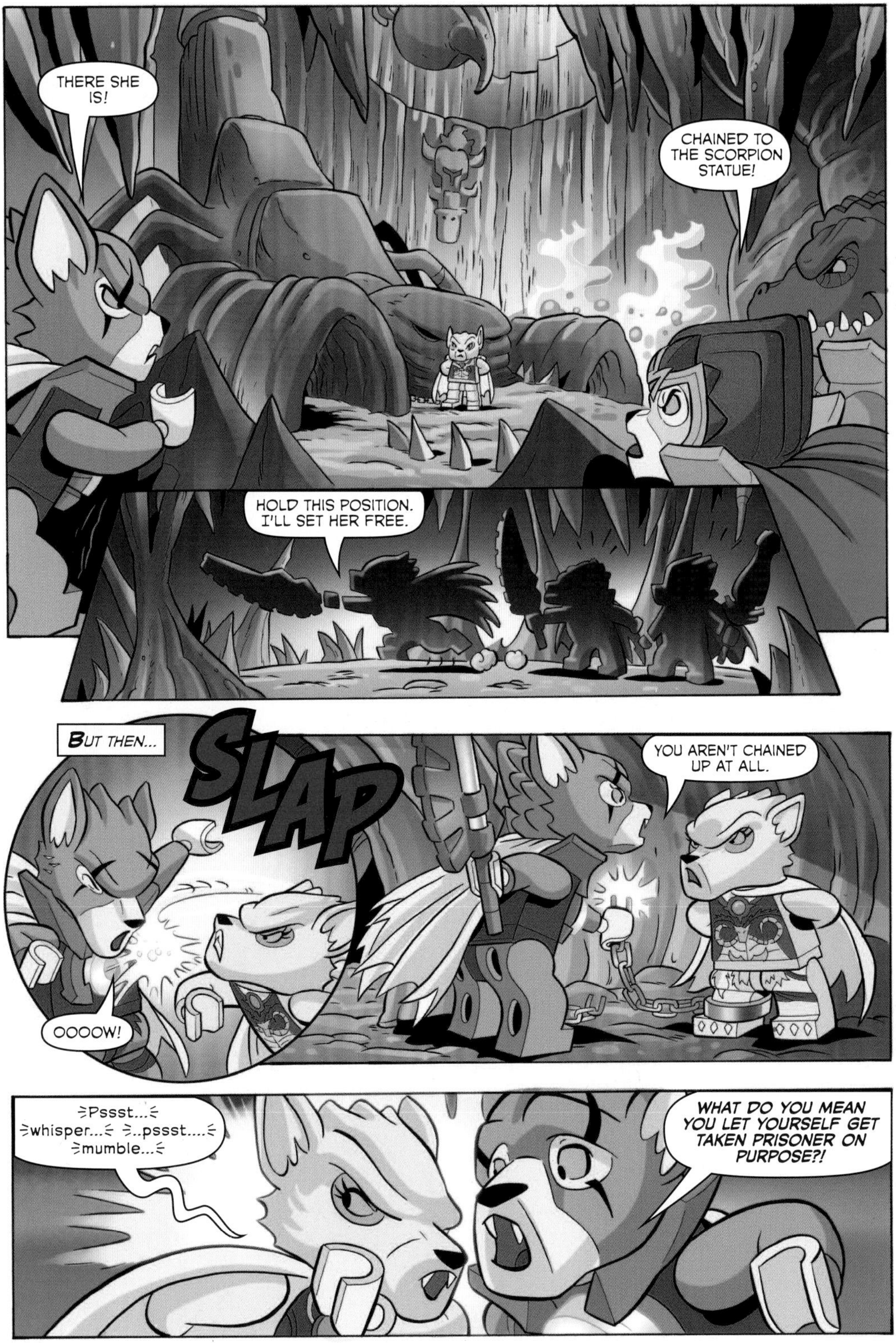
THERE SHE IS!
CHAINED TO THE SCORPION STATUE!
HOLD THIS POSITION. I'LL SET HER FREE.
BUT THEN...
SLAP
OOOOW!
YOU AREN'T CHAINED UP AT ALL.
Pssst... whisper... ..pssst.... mumble...
WHAT DO YOU MEAN YOU LET YOURSELF GET TAKEN PRISONER ON PURPOSE?!

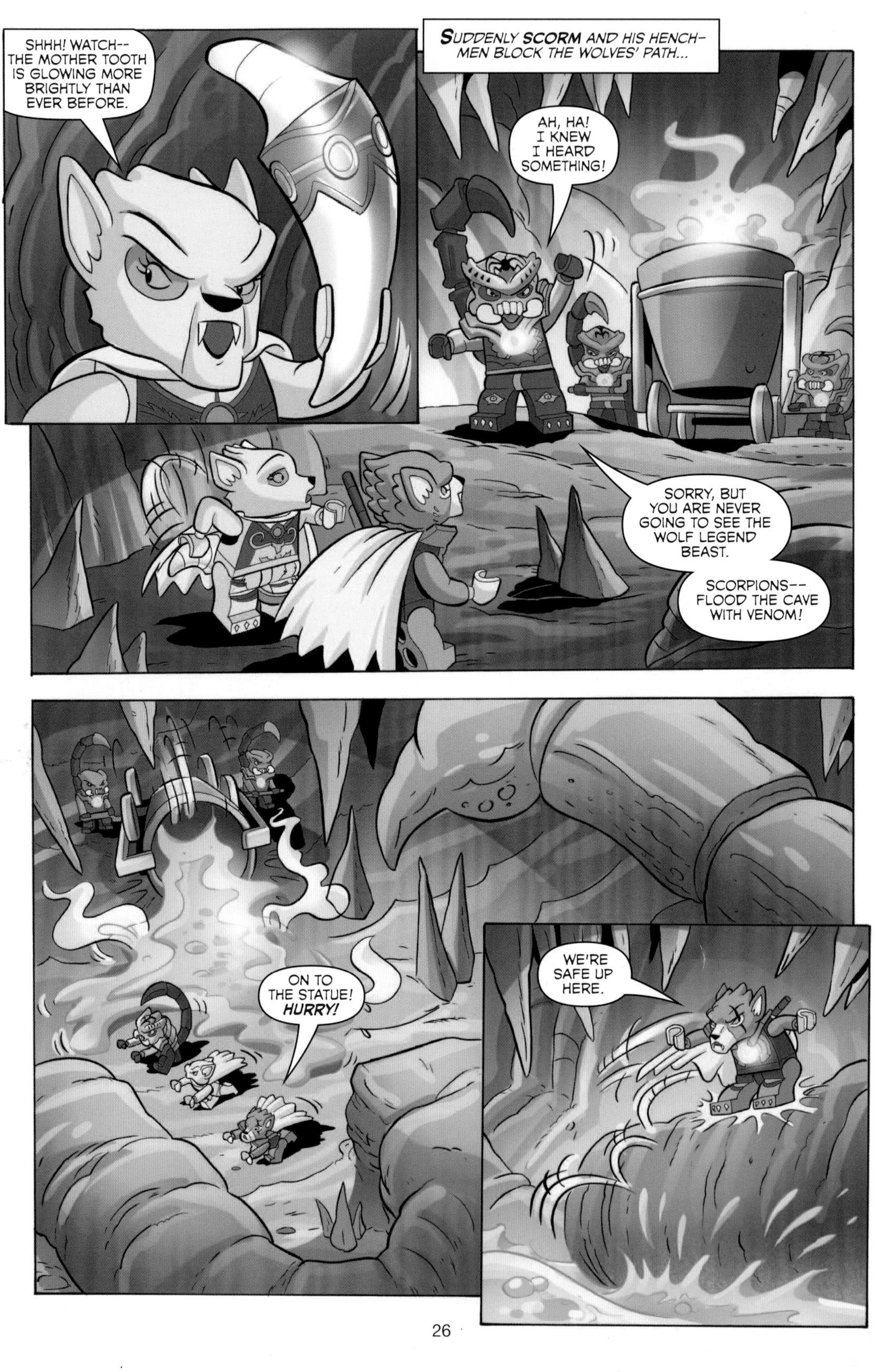
SHHH! WATCH-- THE MOTHER TOOTH IS GLOWING MORE BRIGHTLY THAN EVER BEFORE.
SUDDENLY SCORM AND HIS HENCH-MEN BLOCK THE WOLVES' PATH...
AH, HA! I KNEW I HEARD SOMETHING!
SORRY, BUT YOU ARE NEVER GOING TO SEE THE WOLF LEGEND BEAST.
SCORPIONS-- FLOOD THE CAVE WITH VENOM!
ON TO THE STATUE! HURRY!
WE'RE SAFE UP HERE.

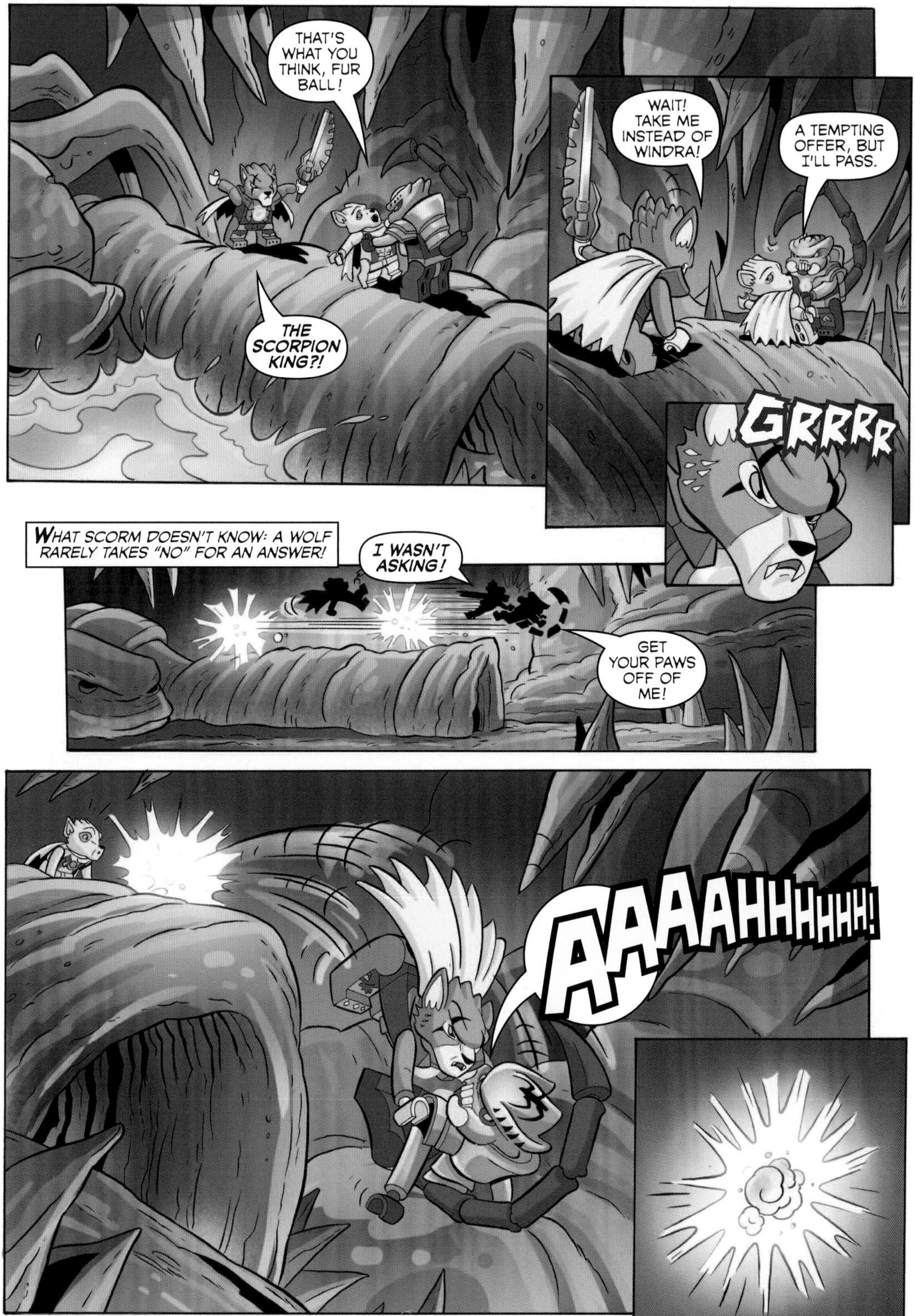
THAT'S WHAT YOU THINK, FUR BALL!
THE SCORPION KING?!
WAIT! TAKE ME INSTEAD OF WINDRA!
A TEMPTING OFFER, BUT I'LL PASS.
GRRRR
WHAT SCORM DOESN'T KNOW: A WOLF RARELY TAKES "NO" FOR AN ANSWER!
I WASN'T ASKING!
GET YOUR PAWS OFF OF ME!
AAAAHHHHHH!

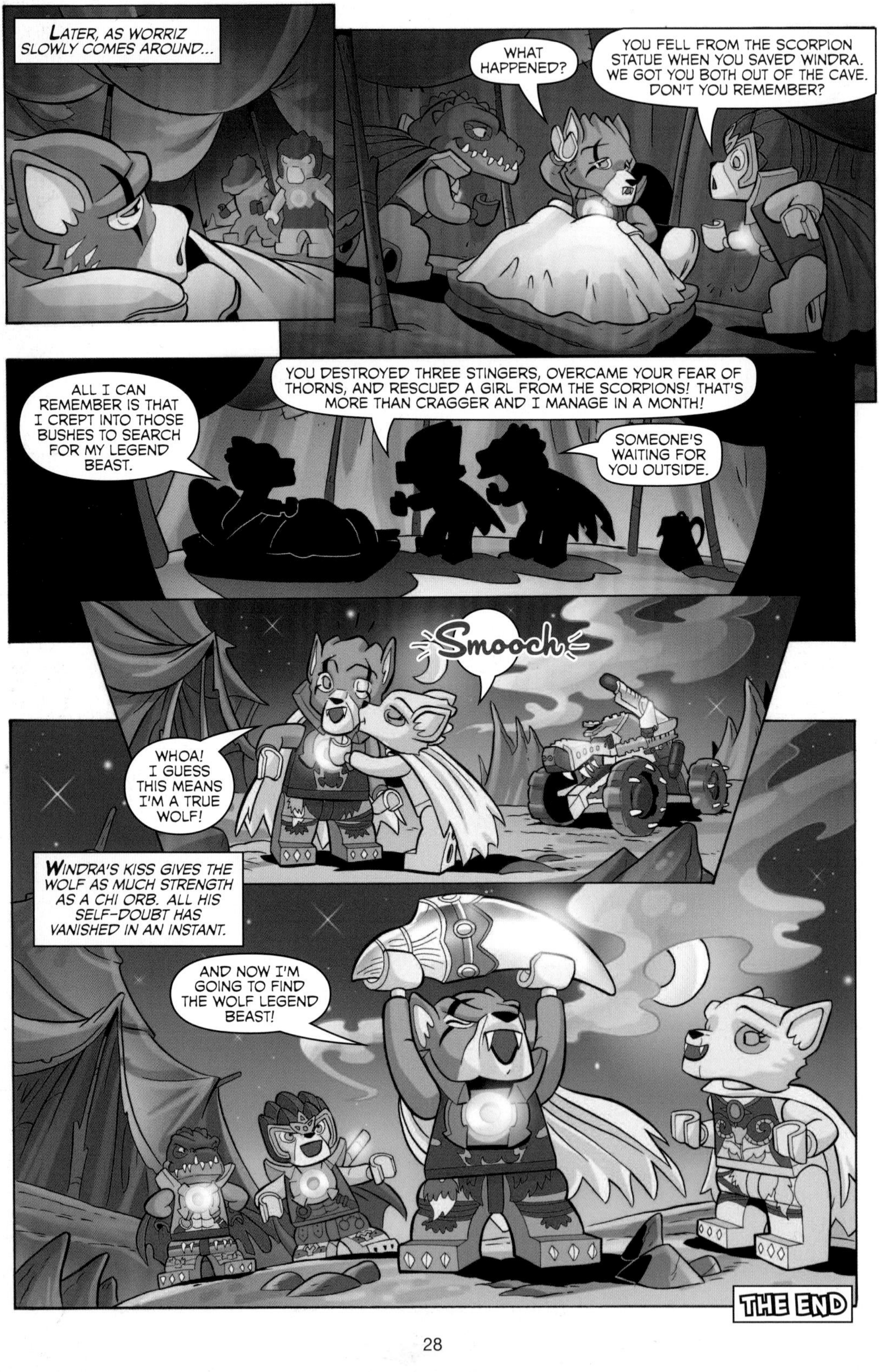
LATER, AS WORRIZ SLOWLY COMES AROUND...
WHAT HAPPENED?
YOU FELL FROM THE SCORPION STATUE WHEN YOU SAVED WINDRA. WE GOT YOU BOTH OUT OF THE CAVE. DON'T YOU REMEMBER?
ALL I CAN REMEMBER IS THAT I CREPT INTO THOSE BUSHES TO SEARCH FOR MY LEGEND BEAST.
YOU DESTROYED THREE STINGERS, OVERCAME YOUR FEAR OF THORNS, AND RESCUED A GIRL FROM THE SCORPIONS! THAT'S MORE THAN CRAGGER AND I MANAGE IN A MONTH!
SOMEONE'S WAITING FOR YOU OUTSIDE.
Smooch
WHOA! I GUESS THIS MEANS I'M A TRUE WOLF!
WINDRA'S KISS GIVES THE WOLF AS MUCH STRENGTH AS A CHI ORB. ALL HIS SELF-DOUBT HAS VANISHED IN AN INSTANT.
AND NOW I'M GOING TO FIND THE WOLF LEGEND BEAST!
THE END

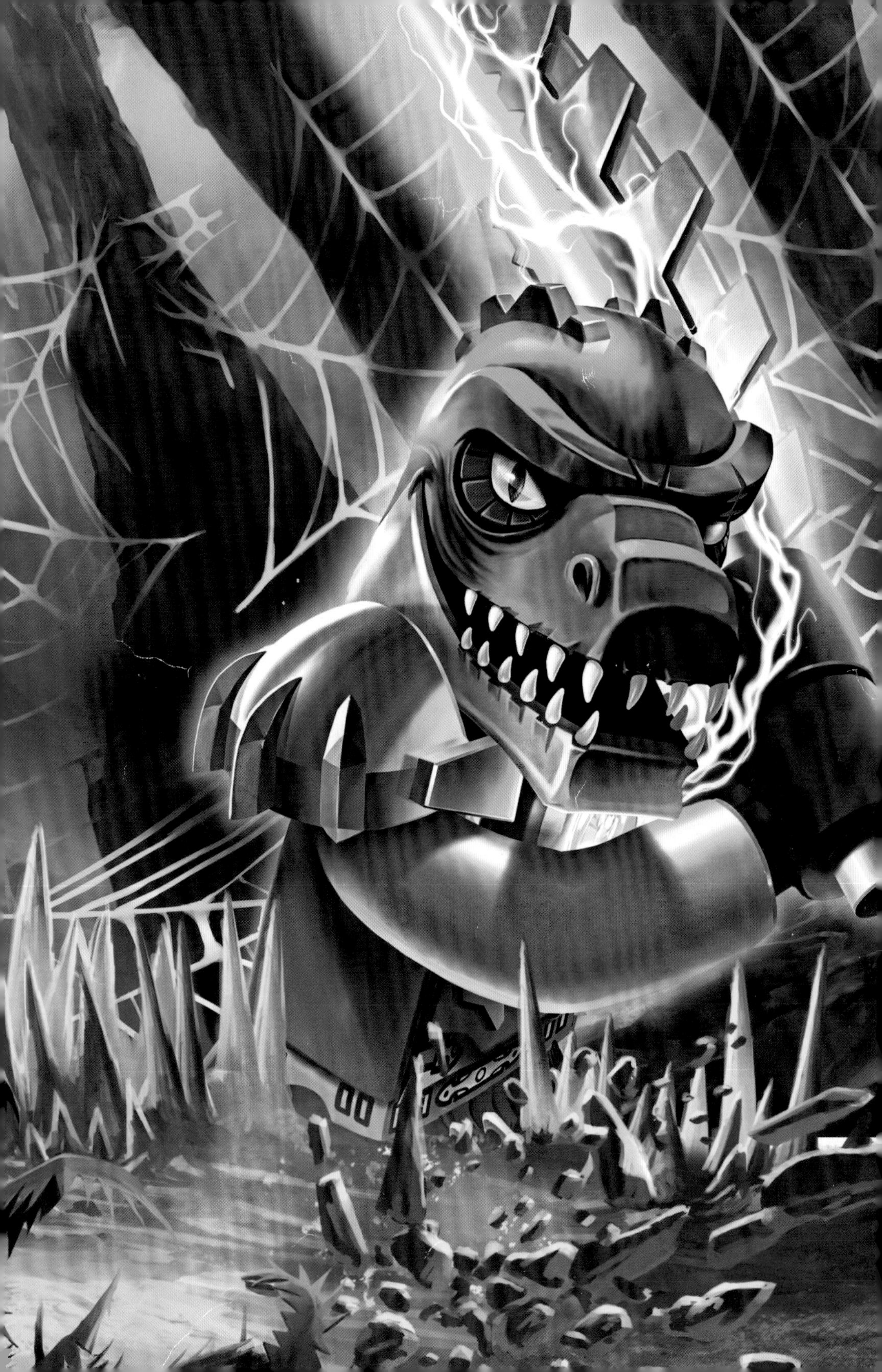

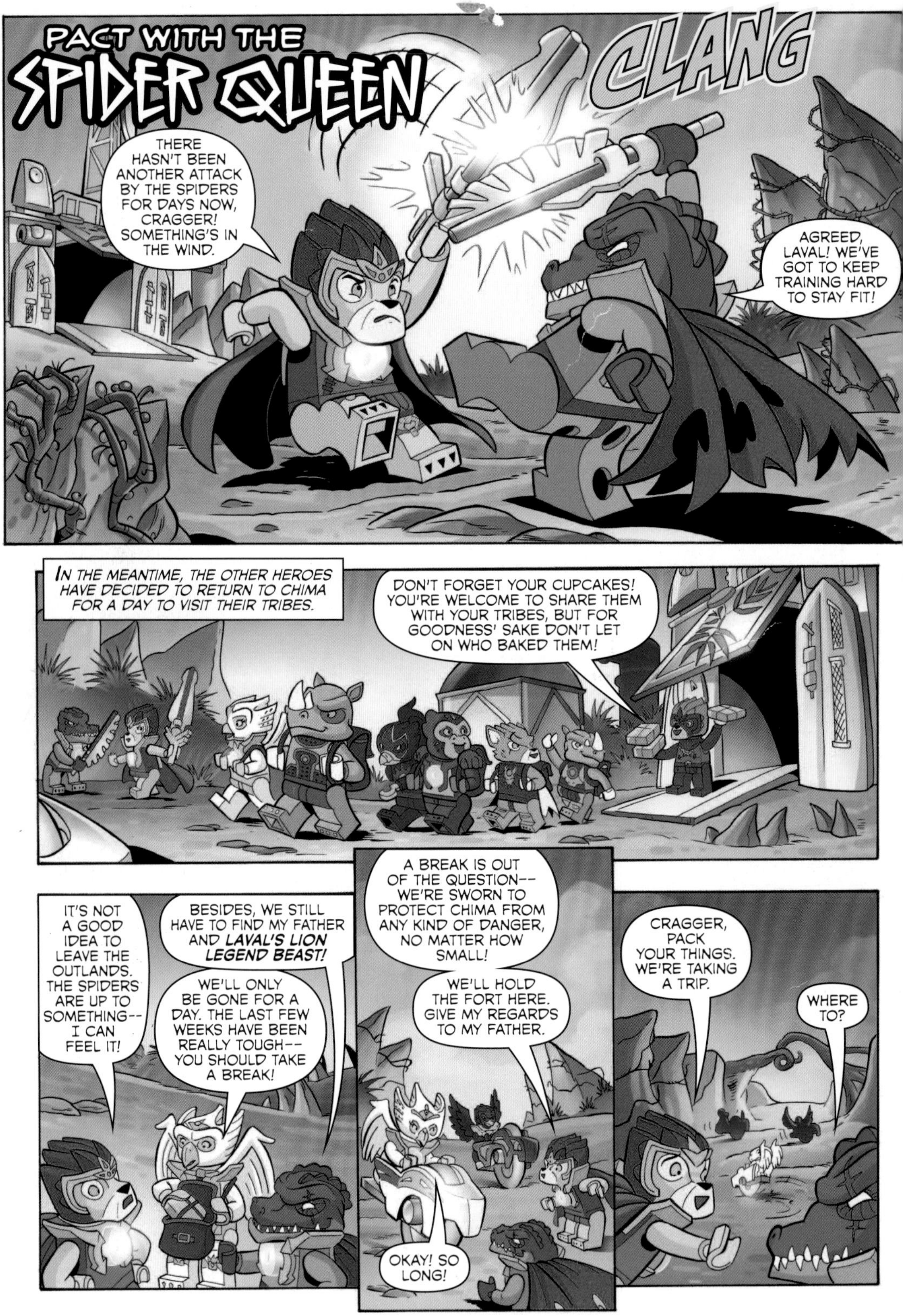
PACT WITH THE SPIDER QUEEN
CLANG
THERE HASN'T BEEN ANOTHER ATTACK BY THE SPIDERS FOR DAYS NOW, CRAGGER! SOMETHING'S IN THE WIND.
AGREED, LAVAL! WE'VE GOT TO KEEP TRAINING HARD TO STAY FIT!
IN THE MEANTIME, THE OTHER HEROES HAVE DECIDED TO RETURN TO CHIMA FOR A DAY TO VISIT THEIR TRIBES.
DON'T FORGET YOUR CUPCAKES! YOU'RE WELCOME TO SHARE THEM WITH YOUR TRIBES, BUT FOR GOODNESS' SAKE DON'T LET ON WHO BAKED THEM!
IT'S NOT A GOOD IDEA TO LEAVE THE OUTLANDS. THE SPIDERS ARE UP TO SOMETHING-- I CAN FEEL IT!
BESIDES, WE STILL HAVE TO FIND MY FATHER AND LAVAL'S LION LEGEND BEAST!
WE'LL ONLY BE GONE FOR A DAY. THE LAST FEW WEEKS HAVE BEEN REALLY TOUGH-- YOU SHOULD TAKE A BREAK!
A BREAK IS OUT OF THE QUESTION-- WE'RE SWORN TO PROTECT CHIMA FROM ANY KIND OF DANGER, NO MATTER HOW SMALL!
WE'LL HOLD THE FORT HERE. GIVE MY REGARDS TO MY FATHER.
OKAY! SO LONG!
CRAGGER, PACK YOUR THINGS. WE'RE TAKING A TRIP.
WHERE TO?

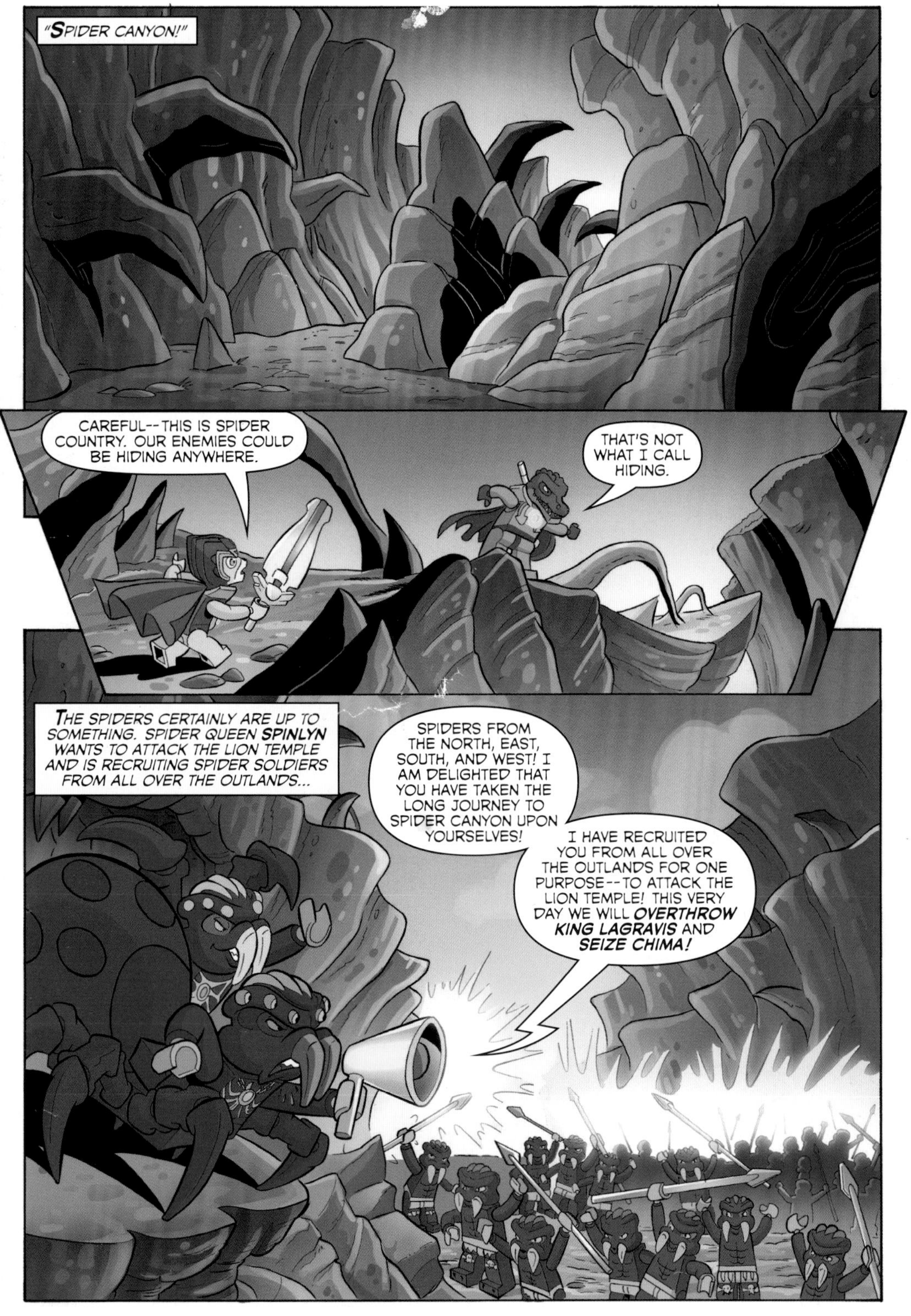
"SPIDER CANYON!"
CAREFUL--THIS IS SPIDER COUNTRY. OUR ENEMIES COULD BE HIDING ANYWHERE.
THAT'S NOT WHAT I CALL HIDING.
THE SPIDERS CERTAINLY ARE UP TO SOMETHING. SPIDER QUEEN SPINLYN WANTS TO ATTACK THE LION TEMPLE AND IS RECRUITING SPIDER SOLDIERS FROM ALL OVER THE OUTLANDS...
SPIDERS FROM THE NORTH, EAST, SOUTH, AND WEST! I AM DELIGHTED THAT YOU HAVE TAKEN THE LONG JOURNEY TO SPIDER CANYON UPON YOURSELVES!
I HAVE RECRUITED YOU FROM ALL OVER THE OUTLANDS FOR ONE PURPOSE--TO ATTACK THE LION TEMPLE! THIS VERY DAY WE WILL OVERTHROW KING LAGRAVIS AND SEIZE CHIMA!

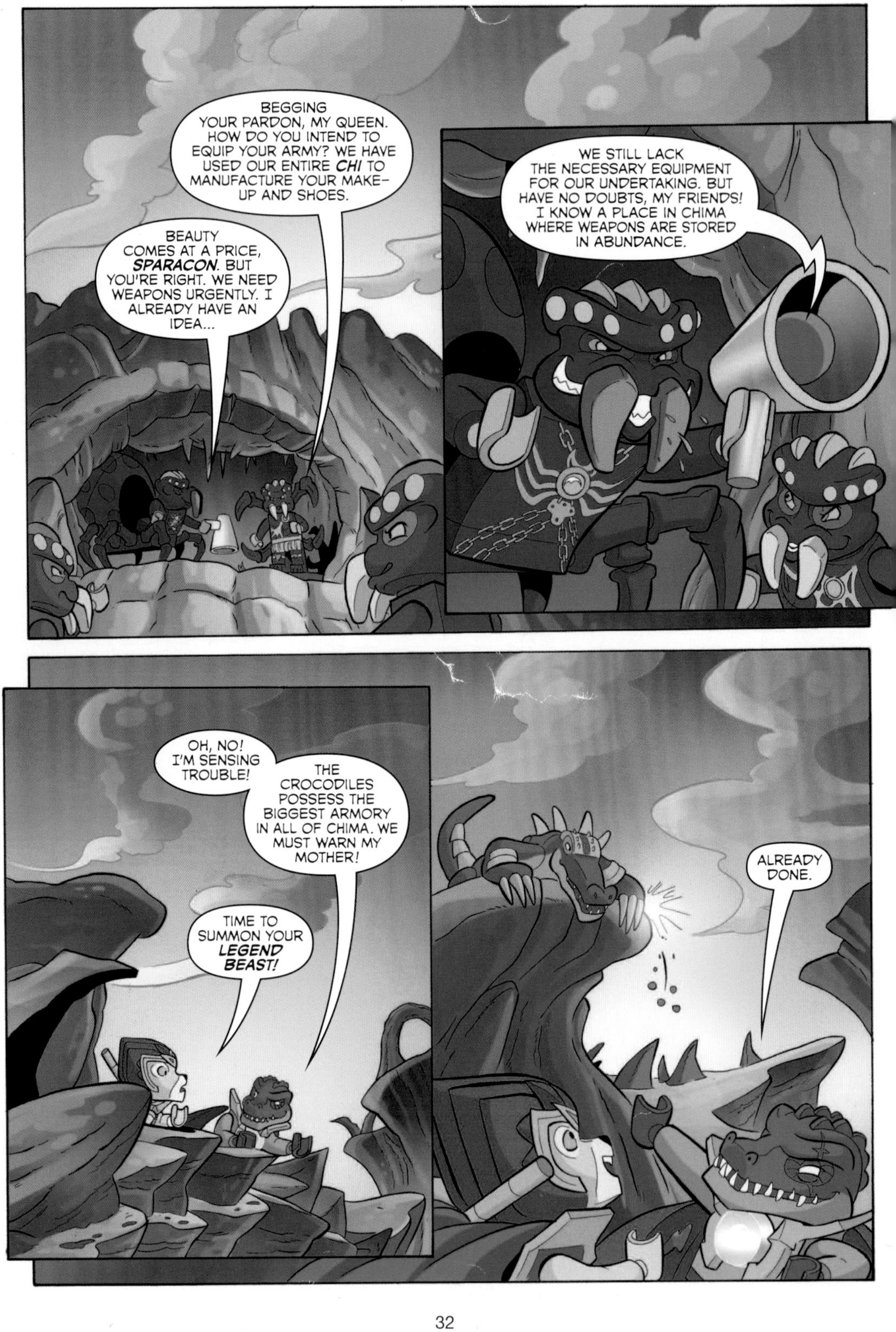
BEGGING YOUR PARDON, MY QUEEN. HOW DO YOU INTEND TO EQUIP YOUR ARMY? WE HAVE USED OUR ENTIRE CHI TO MANUFACTURE YOUR MAKE-UP AND SHOES.
BEAUTY COMES AT A PRICE, SPARACON. BUT YOU'RE RIGHT. WE NEED WEAPONS URGENTLY. I ALREADY HAVE AN IDEA...
WE STILL LACK THE NECESSARY EQUIPMENT FOR OUR UNDERTAKING. BUT HAVE NO DOUBTS, MY FRIENDS! I KNOW A PLACE IN CHIMA WHERE WEAPONS ARE STORED IN ABUNDANCE.
OH, NO! I'M SENSING TROUBLE!
THE CROCODILES POSSESS THE BIGGEST ARMORY IN ALL OF CHIMA. WE MUST WARN MY MOTHER!
TIME TO SUMMON YOUR LEGEND BEAST!
ALREADY DONE.

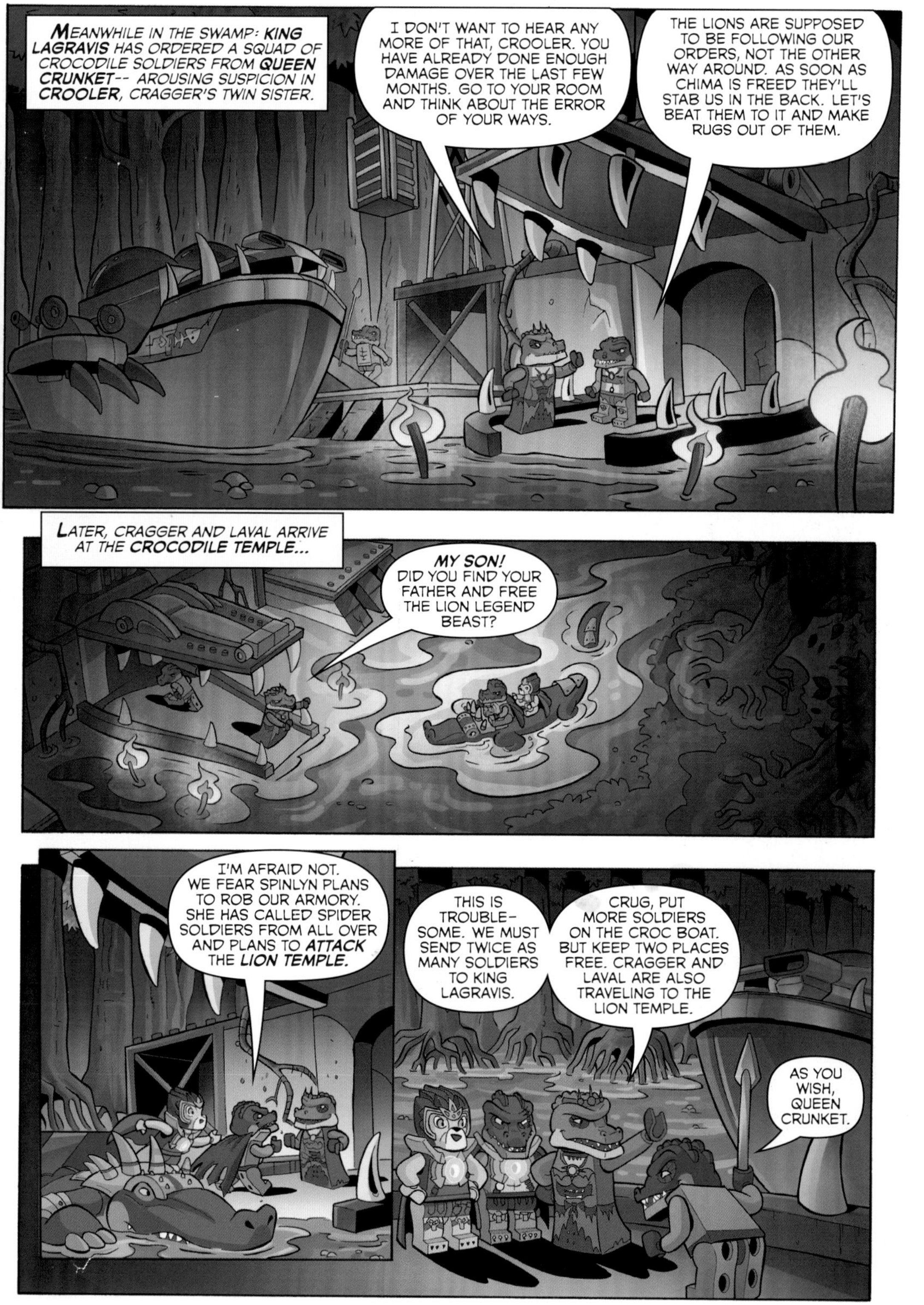
MEANWHILE IN THE SWAMP: KING LAGRAVIS HAS ORDERED A SQUAD OF CROCODILE SOLDIERS FROM QUEEN CRUNKET-- AROUSING SUSPICION IN CROOLER, CRAGGER'S TWIN SISTER.
I DON'T WANT TO HEAR ANY MORE OF THAT, CROOLER. YOU HAVE ALREADY DONE ENOUGH DAMAGE OVER THE LAST FEW MONTHS. GO TO YOUR ROOM AND THINK ABOUT THE ERROR OF YOUR WAYS.
THE LIONS ARE SUPPOSED TO BE FOLLOWING OUR ORDERS, NOT THE OTHER WAY AROUND. AS SOON AS CHIMA IS FREED THEY'LL STAB US IN THE BACK. LET'S BEAT THEM TO IT AND MAKE RUGS OUT OF THEM.
LATER, CRAGGER AND LAVAL ARRIVE AT THE CROCODILE TEMPLE...
MY SON! DID YOU FIND YOUR FATHER AND FREE THE LION LEGEND BEAST?
I'M AFRAID NOT. WE FEAR SPINLYN PLANS TO ROB OUR ARMORY. SHE HAS CALLED SPIDER SOLDIERS FROM ALL OVER AND PLANS TO ATTACK THE LION TEMPLE.
THIS IS TROUBLE-SOME. WE MUST SEND TWICE AS MANY SOLDIERS TO KING LAGRAVIS.
CRUG, PUT MORE SOLDIERS ON THE CROC BOAT. BUT KEEP TWO PLACES FREE. CRAGGER AND LAVAL ARE ALSO TRAVELING TO THE LION TEMPLE.
AS YOU WISH, QUEEN CRUNKET.

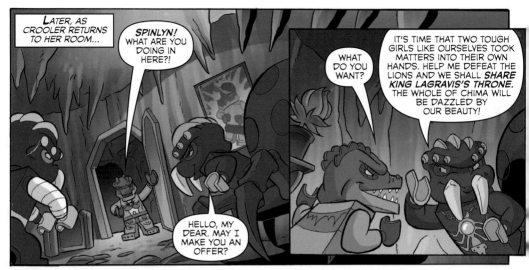

LATER, AS CROOLER RETURNS TO HER ROOM...

SPINLYN! WHAT ARE YOU DOING IN HERE?!

WHAT DO YOU WANT?

HELLO, MY DEAR. MAY I MAKE YOU AN OFFER?

IT'S TIME THAT TWO TOUGH GIRLS LIKE OURSELVES TOOK MATTERS INTO THEIR OWN HANDS. HELP ME DEFEAT THE LIONS AND WE SHALL *SHARE KING LAGRAVIS'S THRONE.* THE WHOLE OF CHIMA WILL BE DAZZLED BY OUR BEAUTY!

NORMALLY I WOULD NEVER ENTER INTO A PACT WITH YOU... BUT IT'S TIME I GOT SOME RESPECT AROUND HERE!

THE SENTINEL STATUE PERMITS ONLY A TRUE CROCODILE TO ENTER THE ARMORY. ANYONE ELSE WILL END UP WITH BROKEN BONES. OR WORSE.

KA-CHING

THIS ARSENAL OF BLASTERS AND GRENADES IS ENOUGH TO ARM THE WHOLE OF CHIMA! THIS IS THE BEGINNING OF A WONDERFUL FRIENDSHIP, MY DEAR.

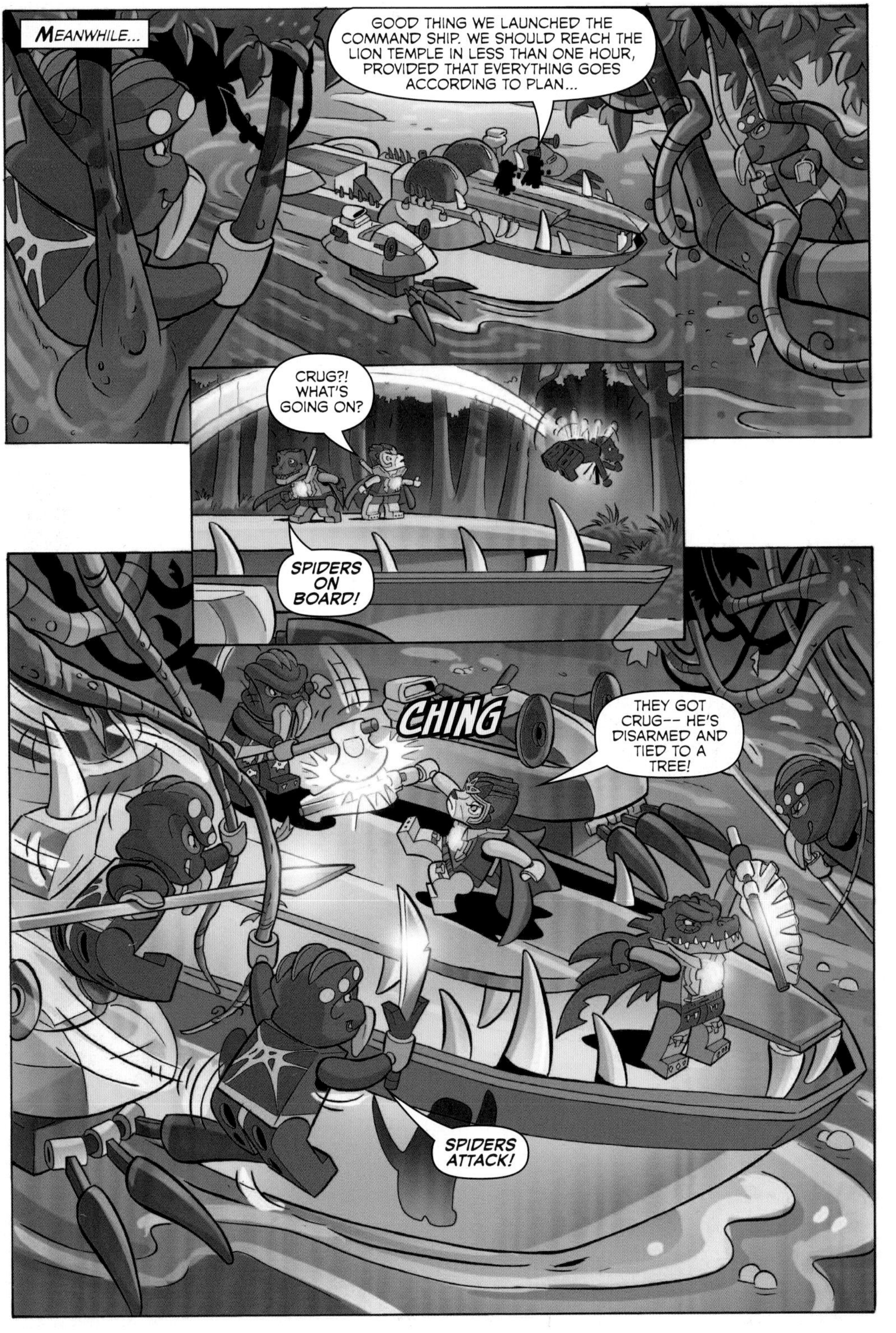
MEANWHILE...
GOOD THING WE LAUNCHED THE COMMAND SHIP. WE SHOULD REACH THE LION TEMPLE IN LESS THAN ONE HOUR, PROVIDED THAT EVERYTHING GOES ACCORDING TO PLAN...
CRUG?! WHAT'S GOING ON?
SPIDERS ON BOARD!
CHING
THEY GOT CRUG-- HE'S DISARMED AND TIED TO A TREE!
SPIDERS ATTACK!

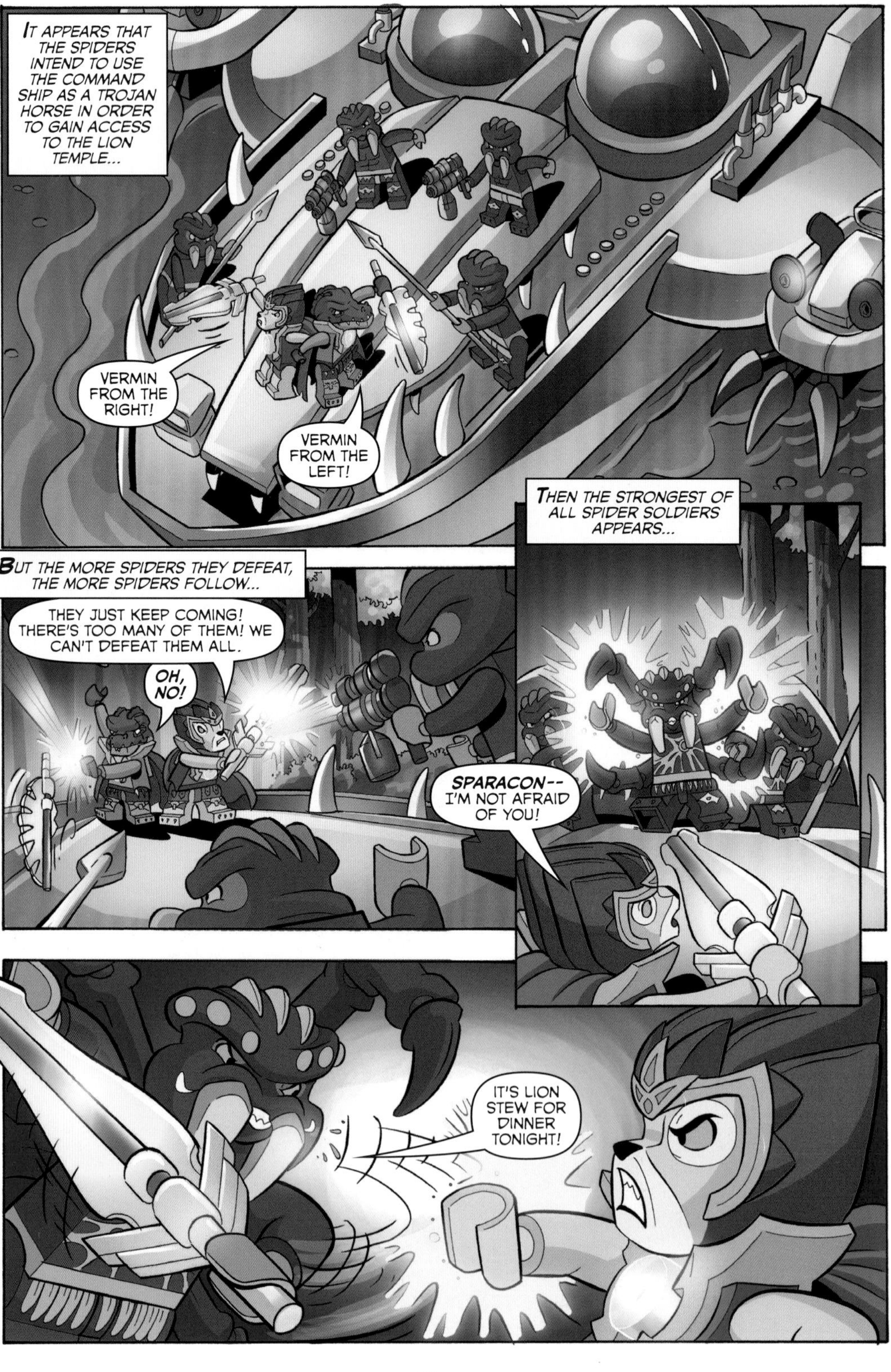
IT APPEARS THAT THE SPIDERS INTEND TO USE THE COMMAND SHIP AS A TROJAN HORSE IN ORDER TO GAIN ACCESS TO THE LION TEMPLE...
VERMIN FROM THE RIGHT!
VERMIN FROM THE LEFT!
BUT THE MORE SPIDERS THEY DEFEAT, THE MORE SPIDERS FOLLOW...
THEY JUST KEEP COMING! THERE'S TOO MANY OF THEM! WE CAN'T DEFEAT THEM ALL.
OH, NO!
THEN THE STRONGEST OF ALL SPIDER SOLDIERS APPEARS...
SPARACON-- I'M NOT AFRAID OF YOU!
IT'S LION STEW FOR DINNER TONIGHT!

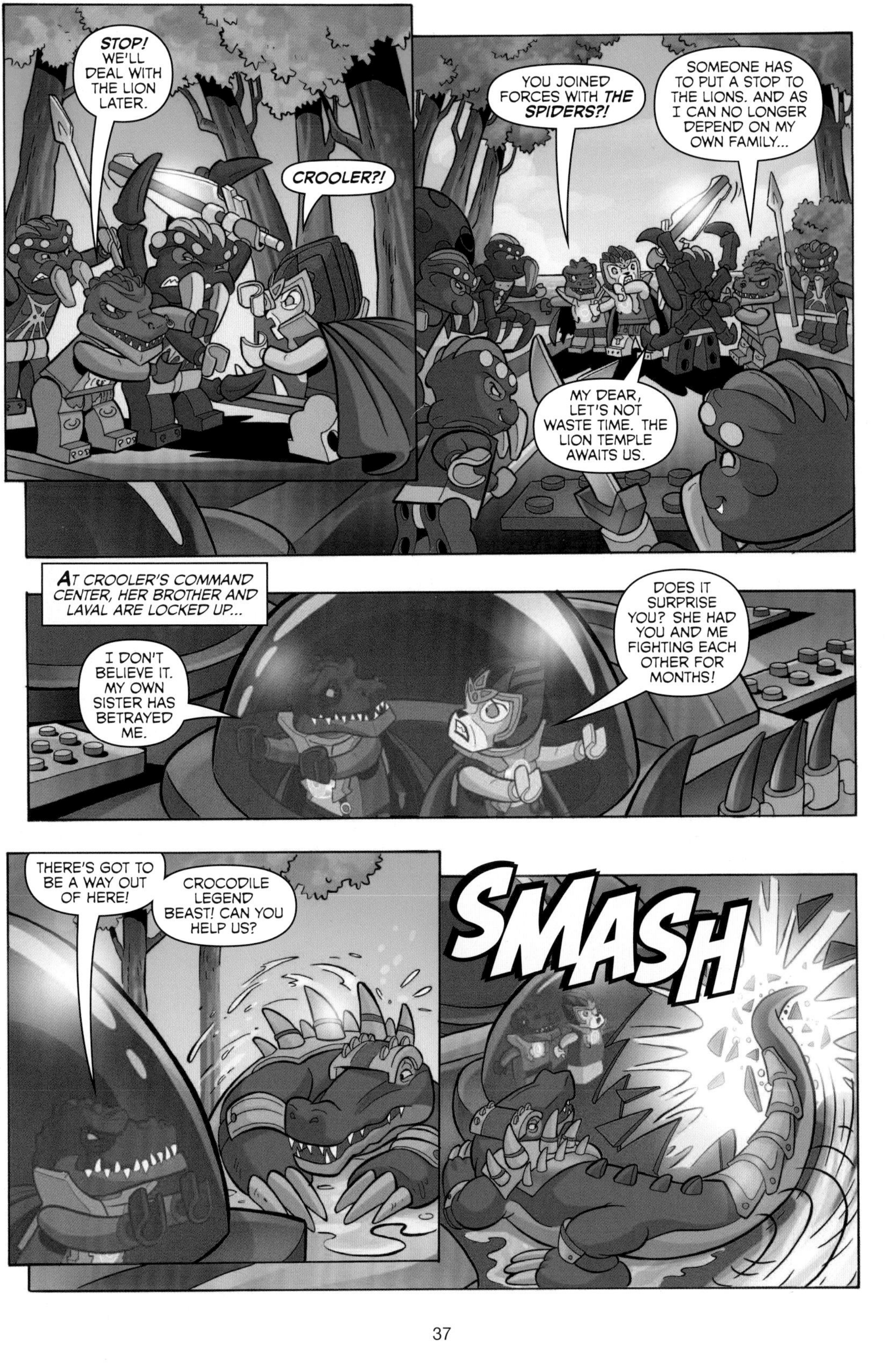
STOP! WE'LL DEAL WITH THE LION LATER.
CROOLER?!
YOU JOINED FORCES WITH THE SPIDERS?!
SOMEONE HAS TO PUT A STOP TO THE LIONS. AND AS I CAN NO LONGER DEPEND ON MY OWN FAMILY...
MY DEAR, LET'S NOT WASTE TIME. THE LION TEMPLE AWAITS US.
AT CROOLER'S COMMAND CENTER, HER BROTHER AND LAVAL ARE LOCKED UP...
I DON'T BELIEVE IT. MY OWN SISTER HAS BETRAYED ME.
DOES IT SURPRISE YOU? SHE HAD YOU AND ME FIGHTING EACH OTHER FOR MONTHS!
THERE'S GOT TO BE A WAY OUT OF HERE!
CROCODILE LEGEND BEAST! CAN YOU HELP US?
SMASH

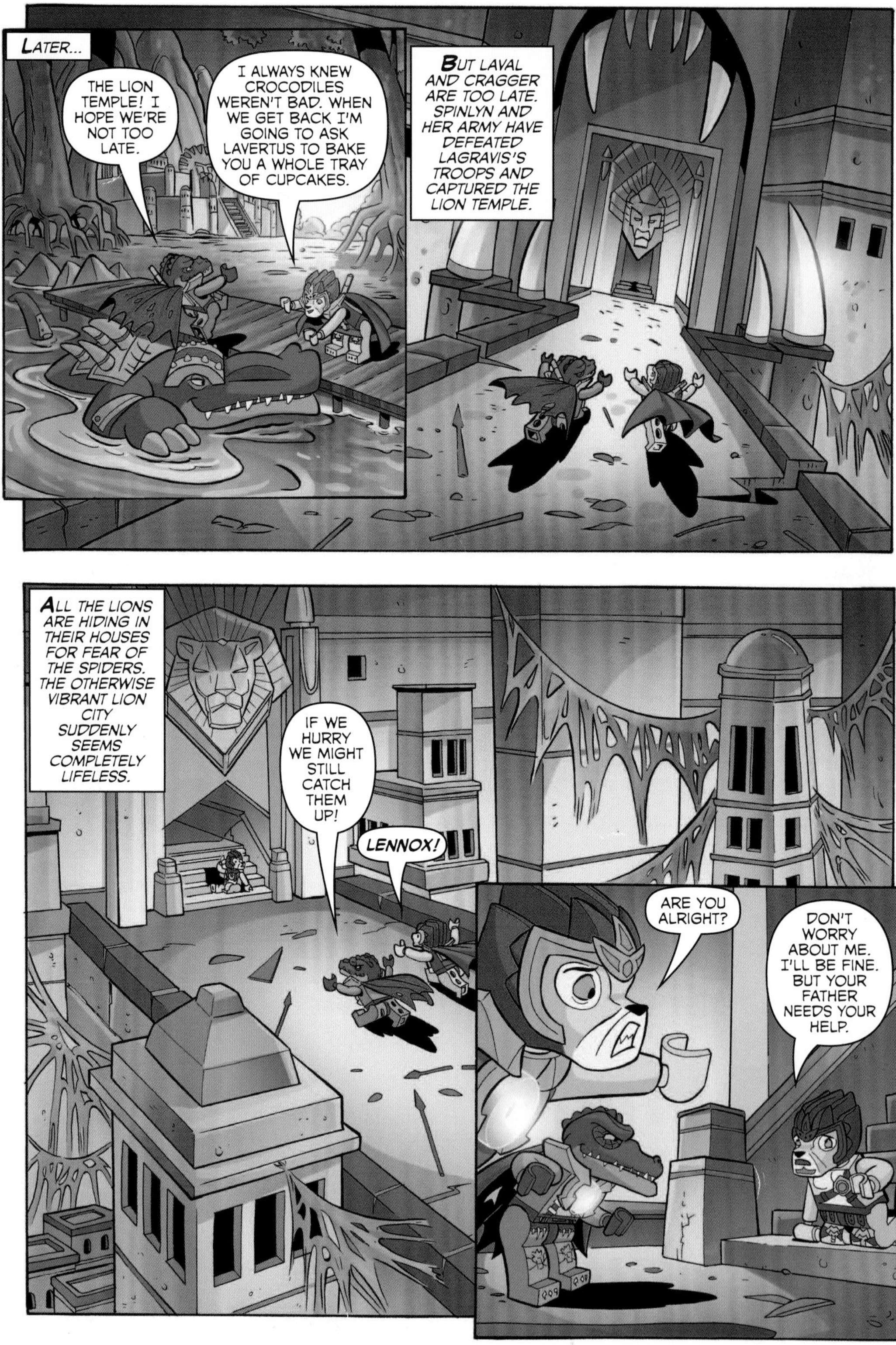
LATER...
THE LION TEMPLE! I HOPE WE'RE NOT TOO LATE.
I ALWAYS KNEW CROCODILES WEREN'T BAD. WHEN WE GET BACK I'M GOING TO ASK LAVERTUS TO BAKE YOU A WHOLE TRAY OF CUPCAKES.
BUT LAVAL AND CRAGGER ARE TOO LATE. SPINLYN AND HER ARMY HAVE DEFEATED LAGRAVIS'S TROOPS AND CAPTURED THE LION TEMPLE.
ALL THE LIONS ARE HIDING IN THEIR HOUSES FOR FEAR OF THE SPIDERS. THE OTHERWISE VIBRANT LION CITY SUDDENLY SEEMS COMPLETELY LIFELESS.
IF WE HURRY WE MIGHT STILL CATCH THEM UP!
LENNOX!
ARE YOU ALRIGHT?
DON'T WORRY ABOUT ME. I'LL BE FINE. BUT YOUR FATHER NEEDS YOUR HELP.

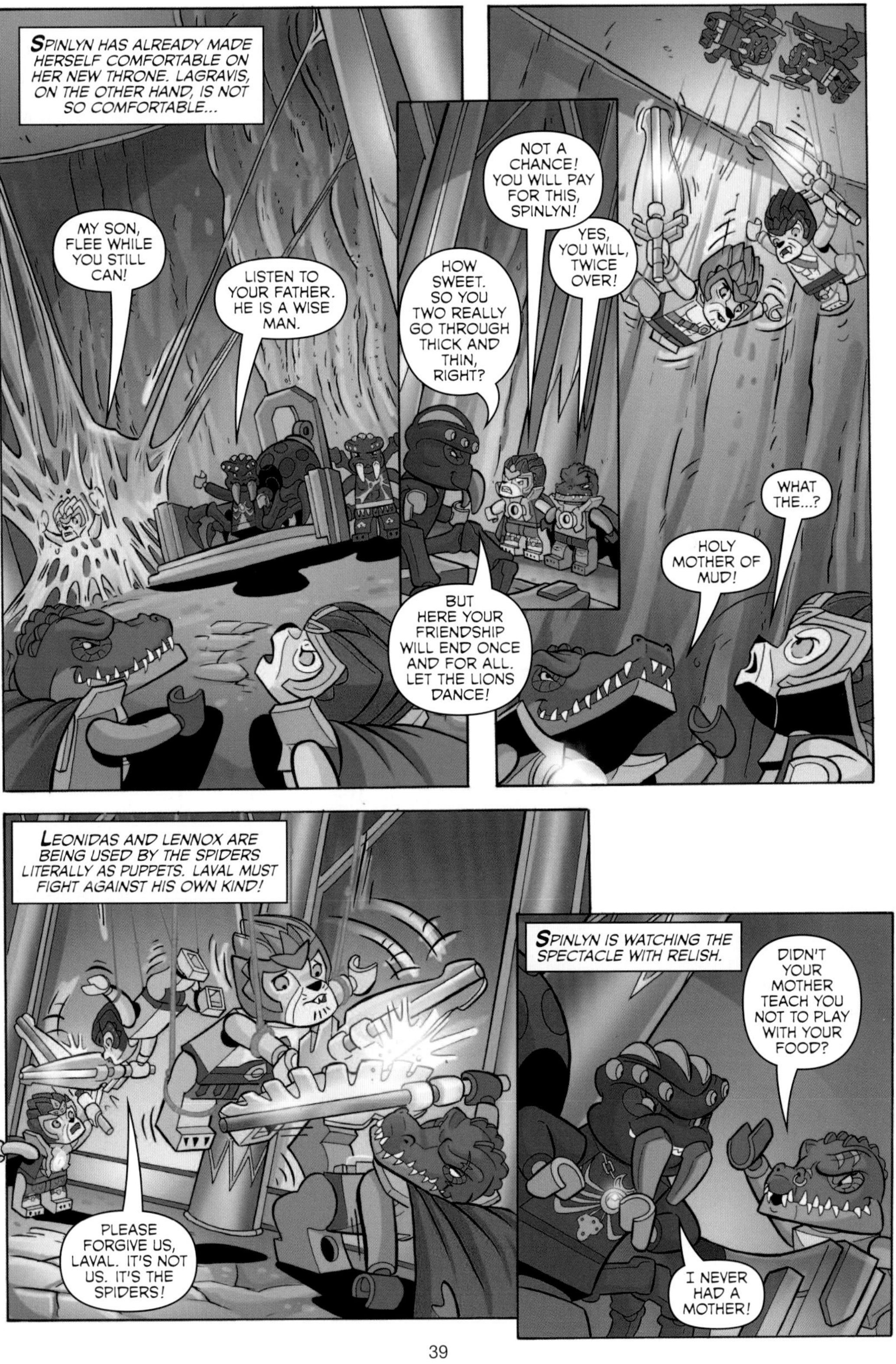
SPINLYN HAS ALREADY MADE HERSELF COMFORTABLE ON HER NEW THRONE. LAGRAVIS, ON THE OTHER HAND, IS NOT SO COMFORTABLE...
MY SON, FLEE WHILE YOU STILL CAN!
LISTEN TO YOUR FATHER. HE IS A WISE MAN.
HOW SWEET. SO YOU TWO REALLY GO THROUGH THICK AND THIN, RIGHT?
NOT A CHANCE! YOU WILL PAY FOR THIS, SPINLYN!
YES, YOU WILL, TWICE OVER!
BUT HERE YOUR FRIENDSHIP WILL END ONCE AND FOR ALL. LET THE LIONS DANCE!
WHAT THE...?
HOLY MOTHER OF MUD!
LEONIDAS AND LENNOX ARE BEING USED BY THE SPIDERS LITERALLY AS PUPPETS. LAVAL MUST FIGHT AGAINST HIS OWN KIND!
PLEASE FORGIVE US, LAVAL. IT'S NOT US. IT'S THE SPIDERS!
SPINLYN IS WATCHING THE SPECTACLE WITH RELISH.
DIDN'T YOUR MOTHER TEACH YOU NOT TO PLAY WITH YOUR FOOD?
I NEVER HAD A MOTHER!

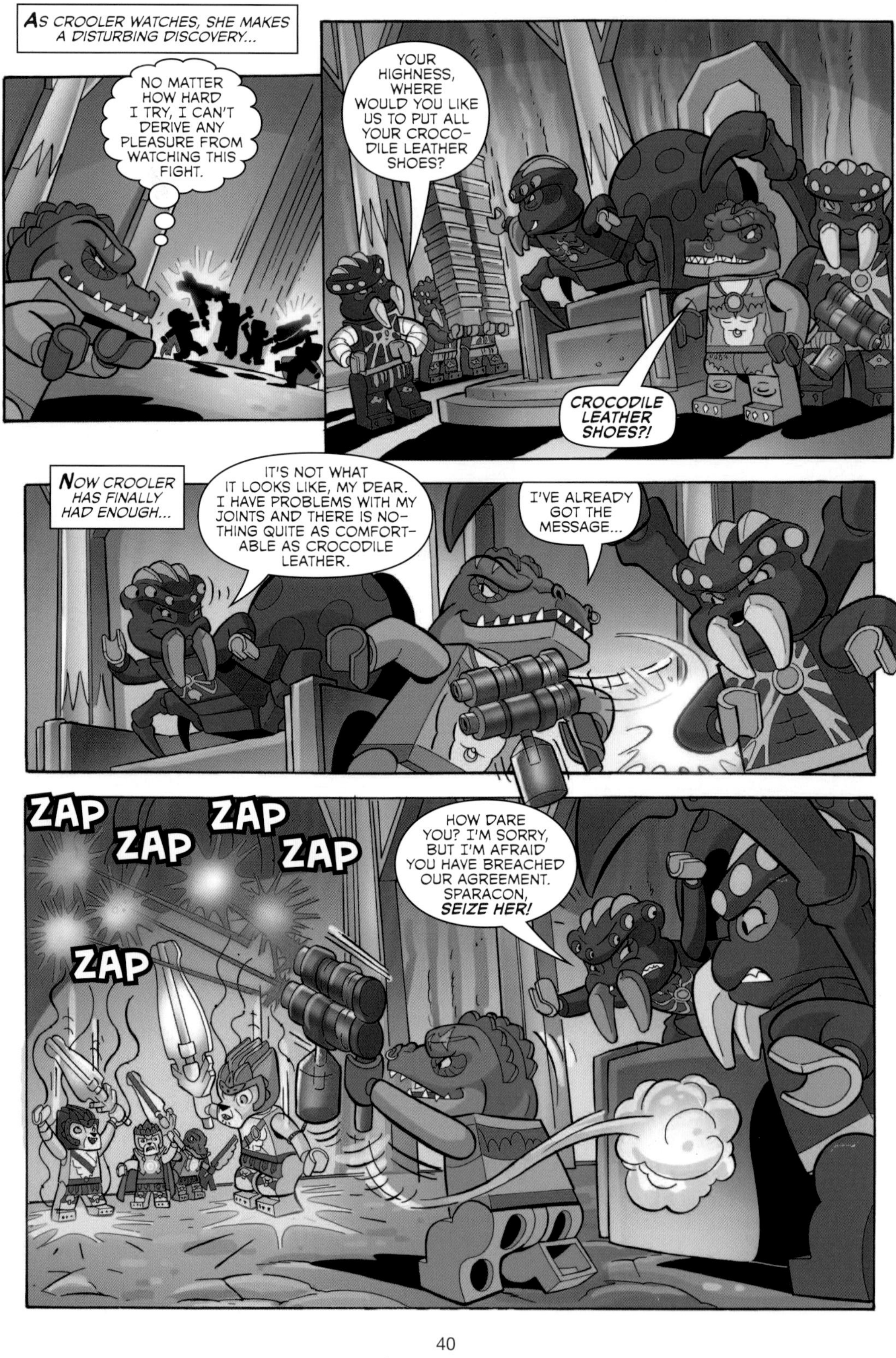

AS CROOLER WATCHES, SHE MAKES A DISTURBING DISCOVERY...
NO MATTER HOW HARD I TRY, I CAN'T DERIVE ANY PLEASURE FROM WATCHING THIS FIGHT.
YOUR HIGHNESS, WHERE WOULD YOU LIKE US TO PUT ALL YOUR CROCO-DILE LEATHER SHOES?
CROCODILE LEATHER SHOES?!
NOW CROOLER HAS FINALLY HAD ENOUGH...
IT'S NOT WHAT IT LOOKS LIKE, MY DEAR. I HAVE PROBLEMS WITH MY JOINTS AND THERE IS NO-THING QUITE AS COMFORT-ABLE AS CROCODILE LEATHER.
I'VE ALREADY GOT THE MESSAGE...
ZAP ZAP ZAP ZAP
ZAP
HOW DARE YOU? I'M SORRY, BUT I'M AFRAID YOU HAVE BREACHED OUR AGREEMENT. SPARACON, SEIZE HER!

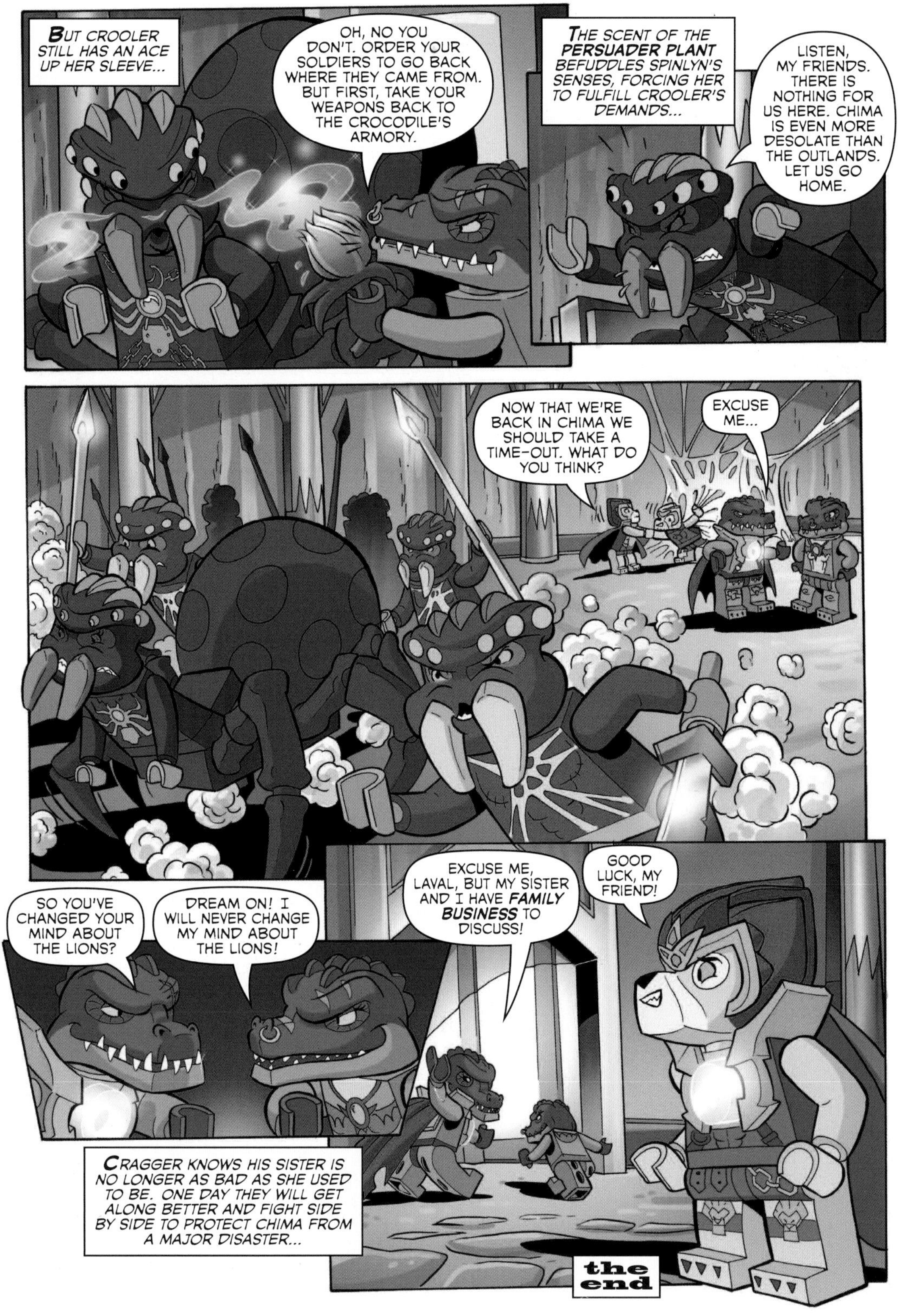
BUT CROOLER STILL HAS AN ACE UP HER SLEEVE...
OH, NO YOU DON'T. ORDER YOUR SOLDIERS TO GO BACK WHERE THEY CAME FROM. BUT FIRST, TAKE YOUR WEAPONS BACK TO THE CROCODILE'S ARMORY.
THE SCENT OF THE PERSUADER PLANT BEFUDDLES SPINLYN'S SENSES, FORCING HER TO FULFILL CROOLER'S DEMANDS...
LISTEN, MY FRIENDS. THERE IS NOTHING FOR US HERE. CHIMA IS EVEN MORE DESOLATE THAN THE OUTLANDS. LET US GO HOME.
NOW THAT WE'RE BACK IN CHIMA WE SHOULD TAKE A TIME-OUT. WHAT DO YOU THINK?
EXCUSE ME...
SO YOU'VE CHANGED YOUR MIND ABOUT THE LIONS?
DREAM ON! I WILL NEVER CHANGE MY MIND ABOUT THE LIONS!
EXCUSE ME, LAVAL, BUT MY SISTER AND I HAVE FAMILY BUSINESS TO DISCUSS!
GOOD LUCK, MY FRIEND!
CRAGGER KNOWS HIS SISTER IS NO LONGER AS BAD AS SHE USED TO BE. ONE DAY THEY WILL GET ALONG BETTER AND FIGHT SIDE BY SIDE TO PROTECT CHIMA FROM A MAJOR DISASTER...
the end

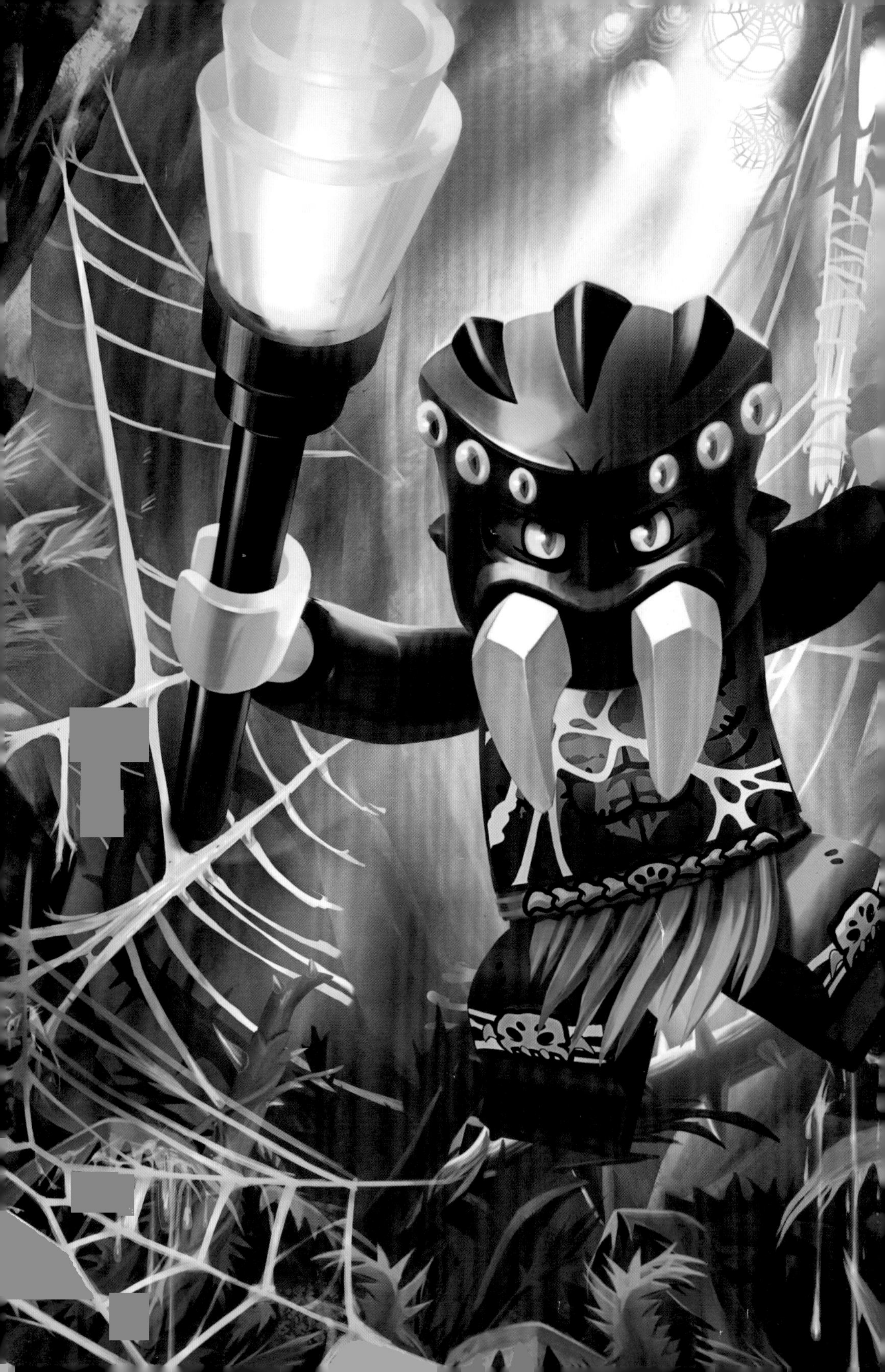

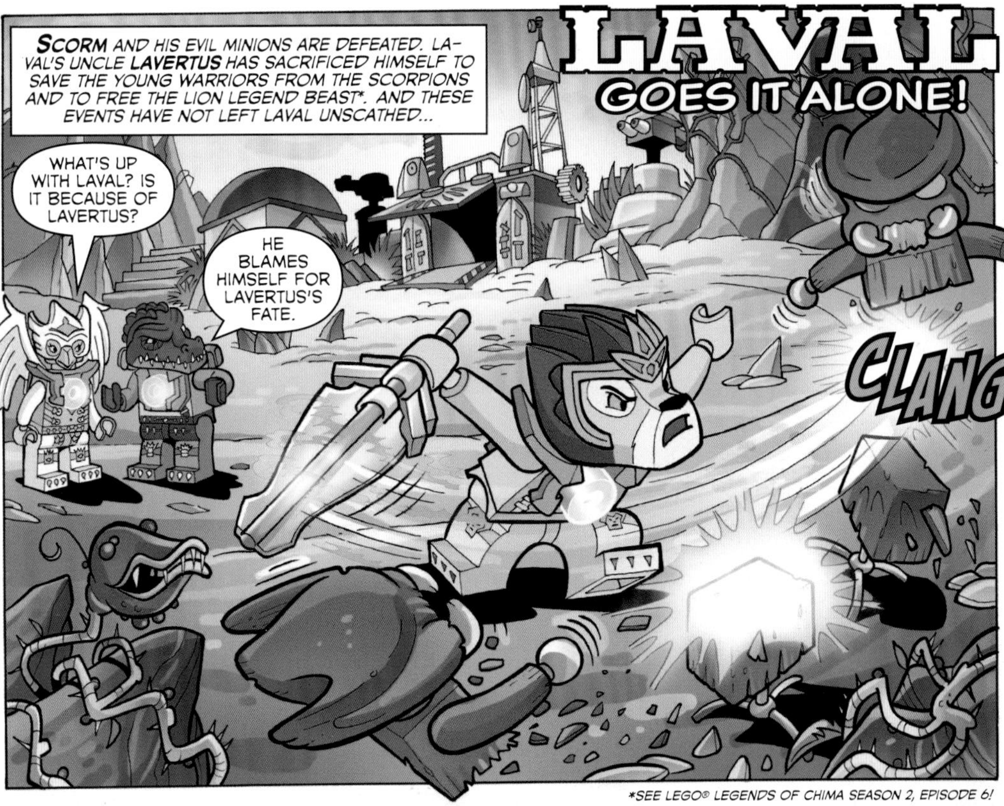
LAVAL
GOES IT ALONE!
SCORM AND HIS EVIL MINIONS ARE DEFEATED. LAVAL'S UNCLE LAVERTUS HAS SACRIFICED HIMSELF TO SAVE THE YOUNG WARRIORS FROM THE SCORPIONS AND TO FREE THE LION LEGEND BEAST*. AND THESE EVENTS HAVE NOT LEFT LAVAL UNSCATHED...
WHAT'S UP WITH LAVAL? IS IT BECAUSE OF LAVERTUS?
HE BLAMES HIMSELF FOR LAVERTUS'S FATE.
CLANG

*SEE LEGO® LEGENDS OF CHIMA SEASON 2, EPISODE 6!

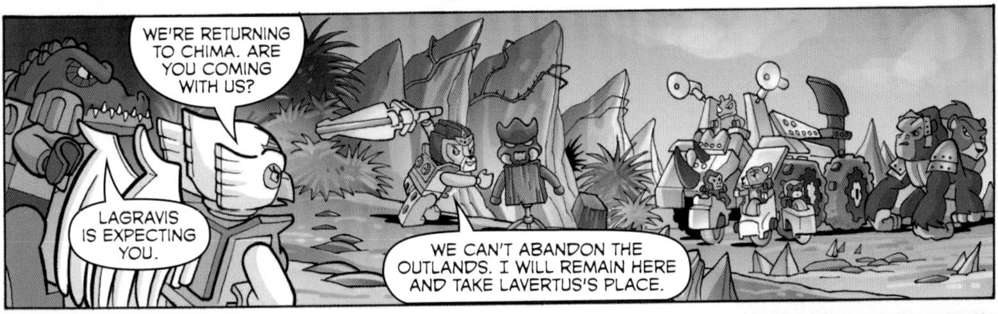
WE'RE RETURNING TO CHIMA. ARE YOU COMING WITH US?
LAGRAVIS IS EXPECTING YOU.
WE CAN'T ABANDON THE OUTLANDS. I WILL REMAIN HERE AND TAKE LAVERTUS'S PLACE.

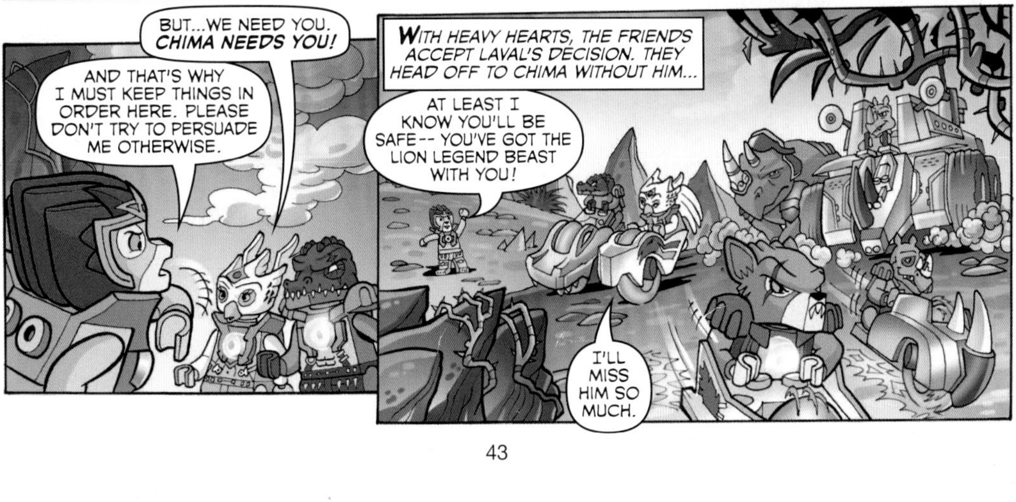
BUT...WE NEED YOU. CHIMA NEEDS YOU!
AND THAT'S WHY I MUST KEEP THINGS IN ORDER HERE. PLEASE DON'T TRY TO PERSUADE ME OTHERWISE.
WITH HEAVY HEARTS, THE FRIENDS ACCEPT LAVAL'S DECISION. THEY HEAD OFF TO CHIMA WITHOUT HIM...
AT LEAST I KNOW YOU'LL BE SAFE-- YOU'VE GOT THE LION LEGEND BEAST WITH YOU!
I'LL MISS HIM SO MUCH.

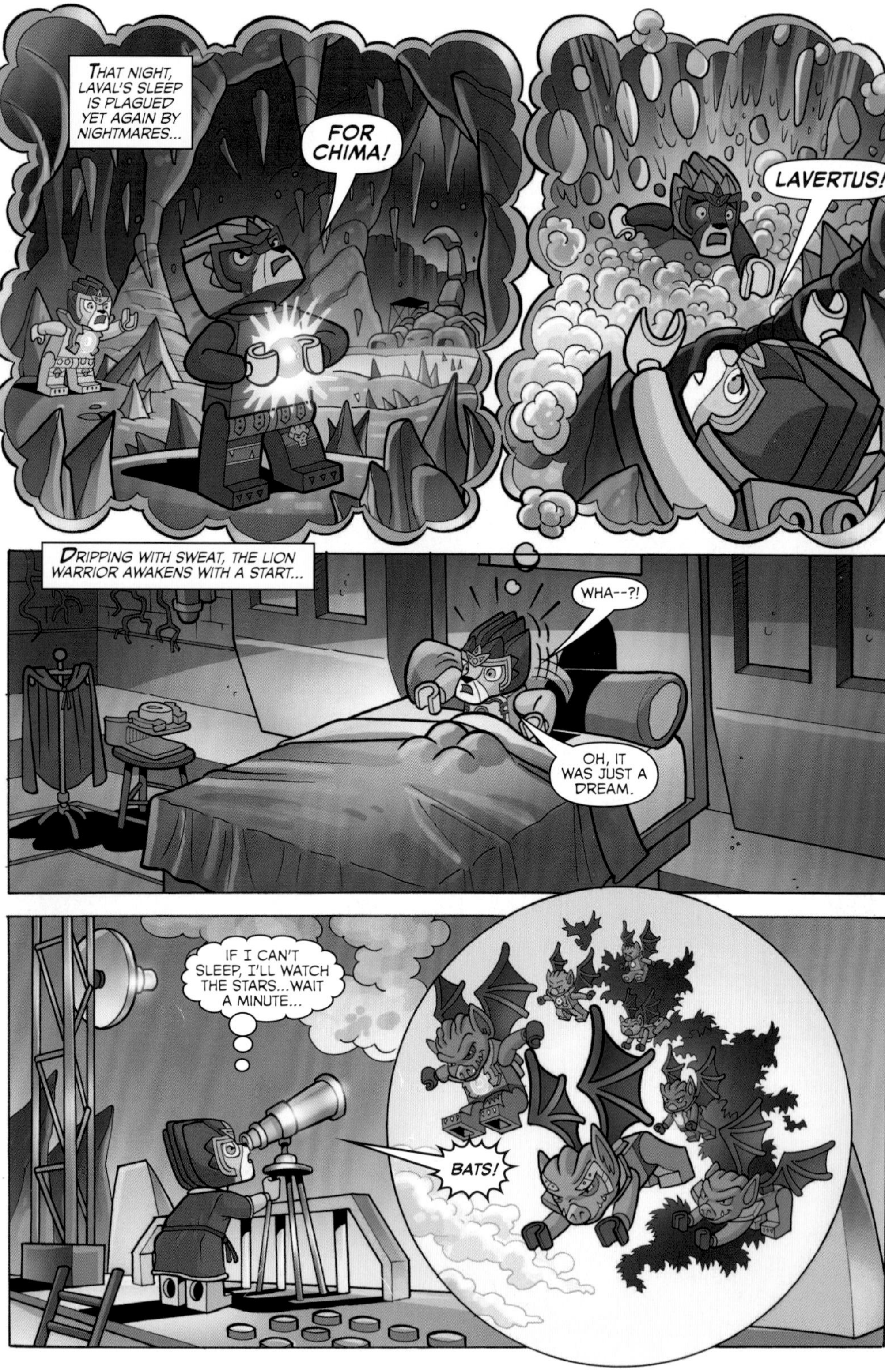
THAT NIGHT, LAVAL'S SLEEP IS PLAGUED YET AGAIN BY NIGHTMARES...
FOR CHIMA!
LAVERTUS!
DRIPPING WITH SWEAT, THE LION WARRIOR AWAKENS WITH A START...
WHA--?!
OH, IT WAS JUST A DREAM.
IF I CAN'T SLEEP, I'LL WATCH THE STARS...WAIT A MINUTE...
BATS!

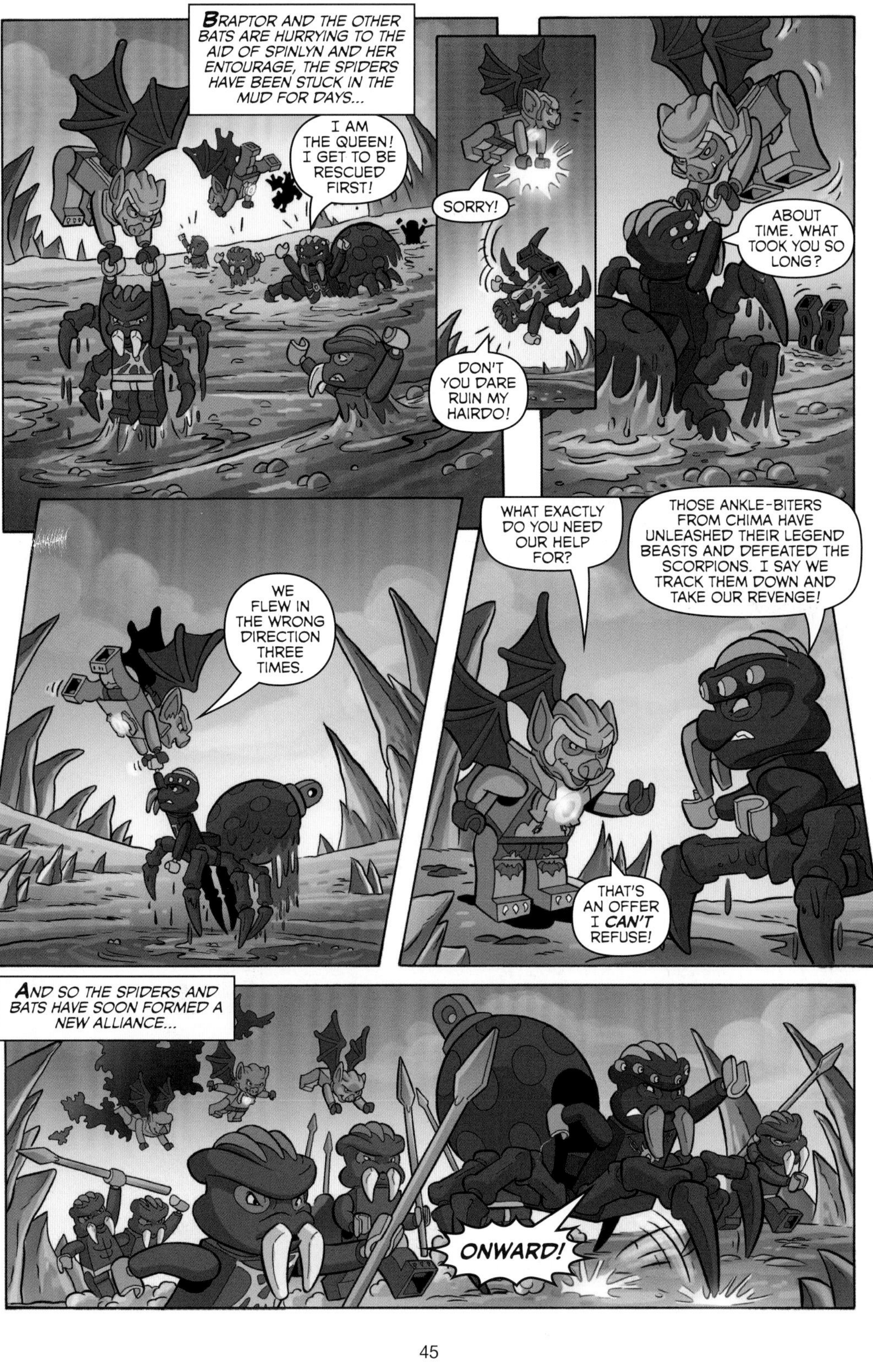
BRAPTOR AND THE OTHER BATS ARE HURRYING TO THE AID OF SPINLYN AND HER ENTOURAGE, THE SPIDERS HAVE BEEN STUCK IN THE MUD FOR DAYS...
I AM THE QUEEN! I GET TO BE RESCUED FIRST!
SORRY!
DON'T YOU DARE RUIN MY HAIRDO!
ABOUT TIME. WHAT TOOK YOU SO LONG?
WE FLEW IN THE WRONG DIRECTION THREE TIMES.
WHAT EXACTLY DO YOU NEED OUR HELP FOR?
THOSE ANKLE-BITERS FROM CHIMA HAVE UNLEASHED THEIR LEGEND BEASTS AND DEFEATED THE SCORPIONS. I SAY WE TRACK THEM DOWN AND TAKE OUR REVENGE!
THAT'S AN OFFER I CAN'T REFUSE!
AND SO THE SPIDERS AND BATS HAVE SOON FORMED A NEW ALLIANCE...
ONWARD!

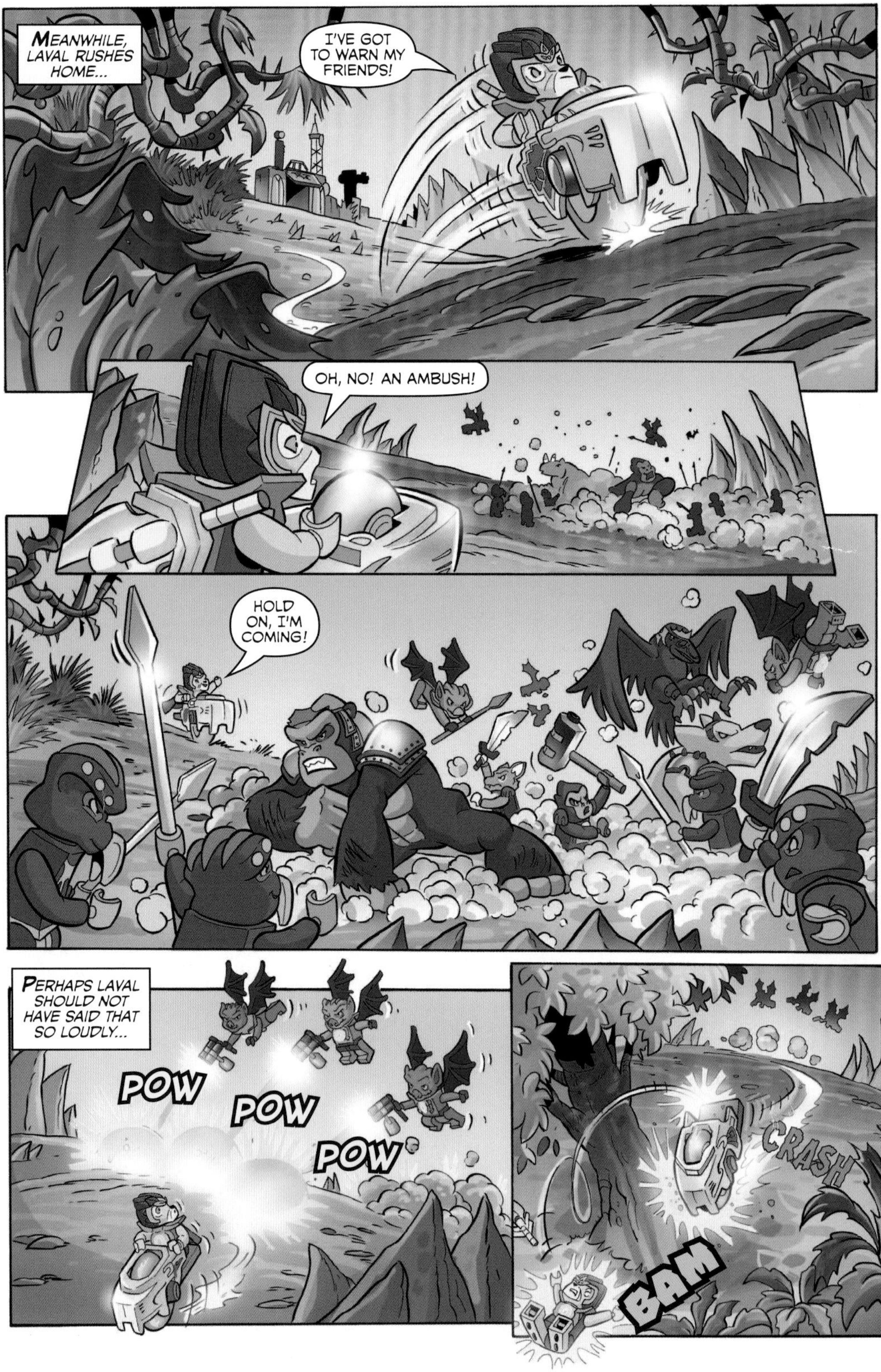
MEANWHILE, LAVAL RUSHES HOME...
I'VE GOT TO WARN MY FRIENDS!
OH, NO! AN AMBUSH!
HOLD ON, I'M COMING!
PERHAPS LAVAL SHOULD NOT HAVE SAID THAT SO LOUDLY...
POW
POW
POW
CRASH
BAM

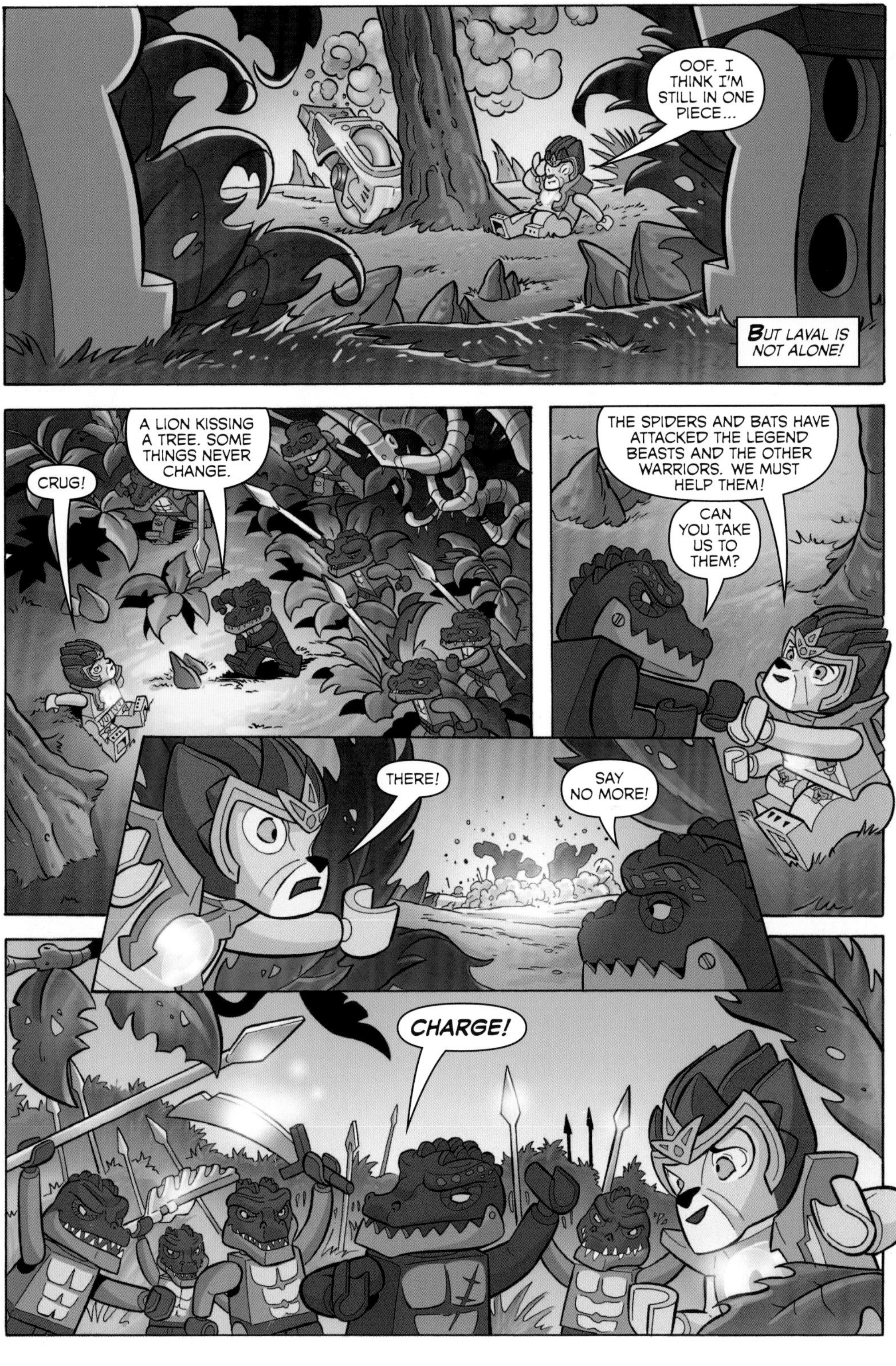
OOF. I THINK I'M STILL IN ONE PIECE...
BUT LAVAL IS NOT ALONE!
CRUG!
A LION KISSING A TREE. SOME THINGS NEVER CHANGE.
THE SPIDERS AND BATS HAVE ATTACKED THE LEGEND BEASTS AND THE OTHER WARRIORS. WE MUST HELP THEM!
CAN YOU TAKE US TO THEM?
THERE!
SAY NO MORE!
CHARGE!

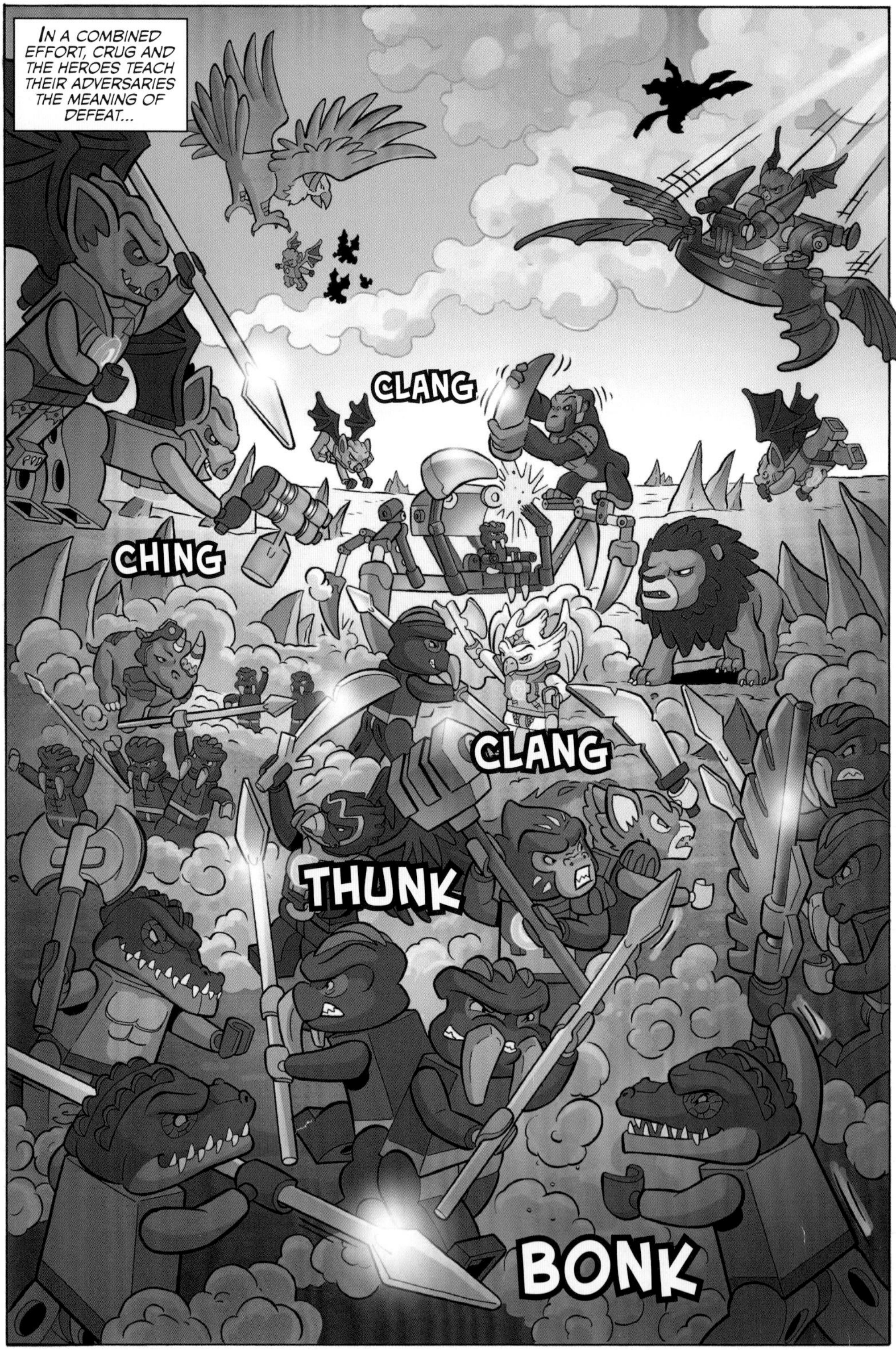
In a combined effort, Crug and the heroes teach their adversaries the meaning of defeat...
CLANG
CHING
CLANG
THUNK
BONK

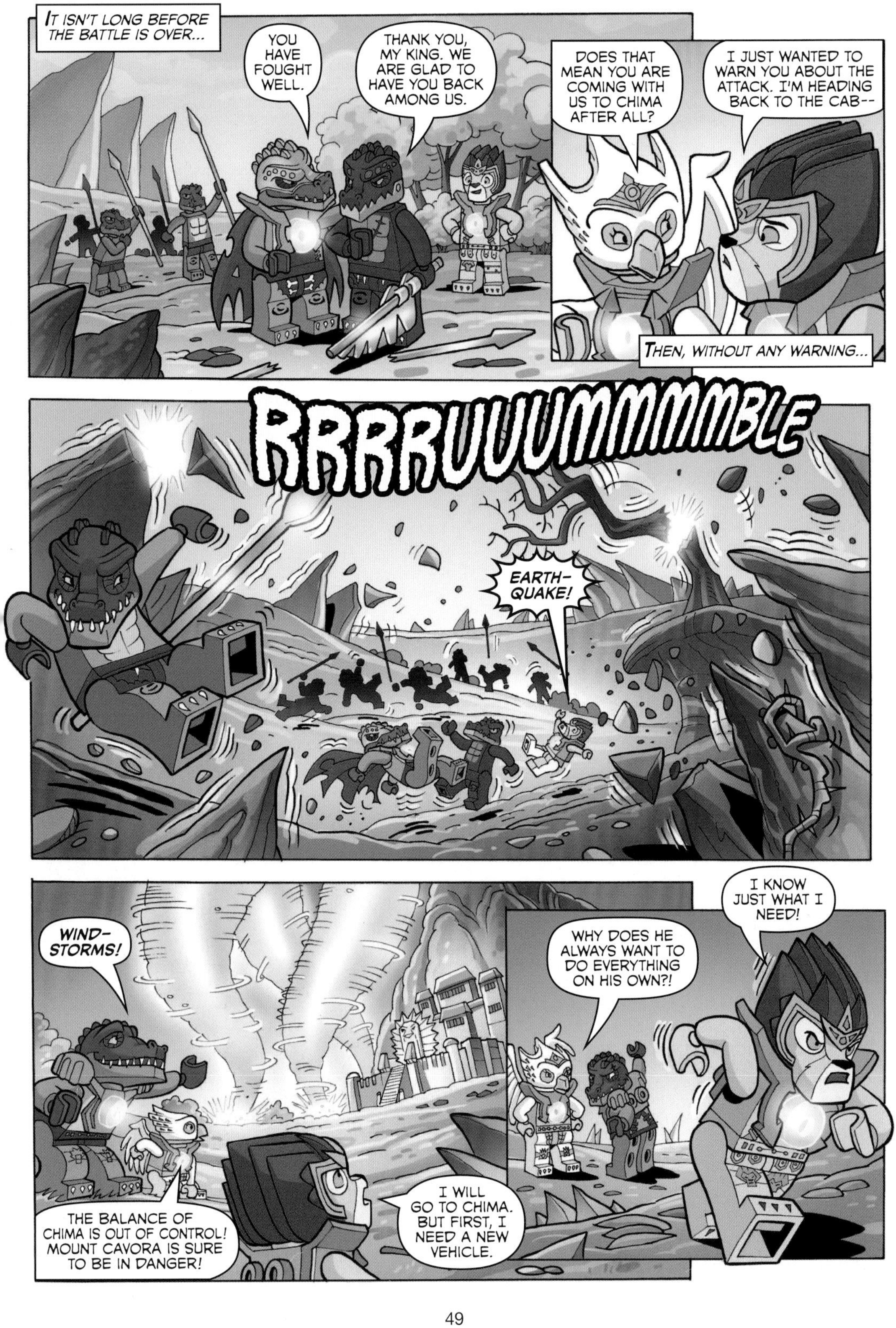
IT ISN'T LONG BEFORE THE BATTLE IS OVER...
YOU HAVE FOUGHT WELL.
THANK YOU, MY KING. WE ARE GLAD TO HAVE YOU BACK AMONG US.
DOES THAT MEAN YOU ARE COMING WITH US TO CHIMA AFTER ALL?
I JUST WANTED TO WARN YOU ABOUT THE ATTACK. I'M HEADING BACK TO THE CAB--
THEN, WITHOUT ANY WARNING...
RRRRUUUMMMMMBLE
EARTH-QUAKE!
WIND-STORMS!
THE BALANCE OF CHIMA IS OUT OF CONTROL! MOUNT CAVORA IS SURE TO BE IN DANGER!
I WILL GO TO CHIMA. BUT FIRST, I NEED A NEW VEHICLE.
WHY DOES HE ALWAYS WANT TO DO EVERYTHING ON HIS OWN?!
I KNOW JUST WHAT I NEED!

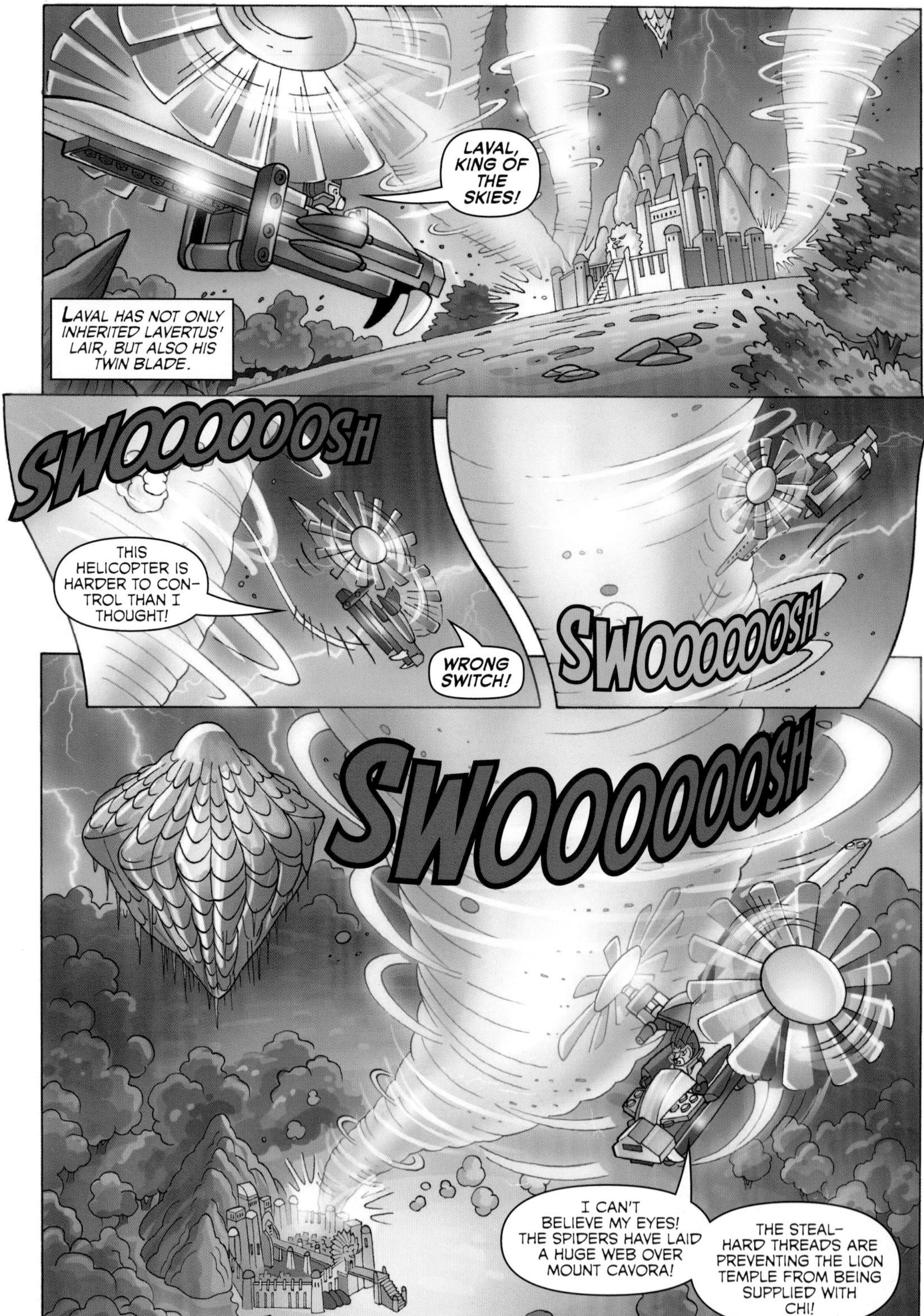
LAVAL, KING OF THE SKIES!
LAVAL HAS NOT ONLY INHERITED LAVERTUS' LAIR, BUT ALSO HIS TWIN BLADE.
SWOOOOOOOSH
THIS HELICOPTER IS HARDER TO CONTROL THAN I THOUGHT!
WRONG SWITCH!
SWOOOOOOOSH
SWOOOOOOOSH
I CAN'T BELIEVE MY EYES! THE SPIDERS HAVE LAID A HUGE WEB OVER MOUNT CAVORA!
THE STEAL-HARD THREADS ARE PREVENTING THE LION TEMPLE FROM BEING SUPPLIED WITH CHI!

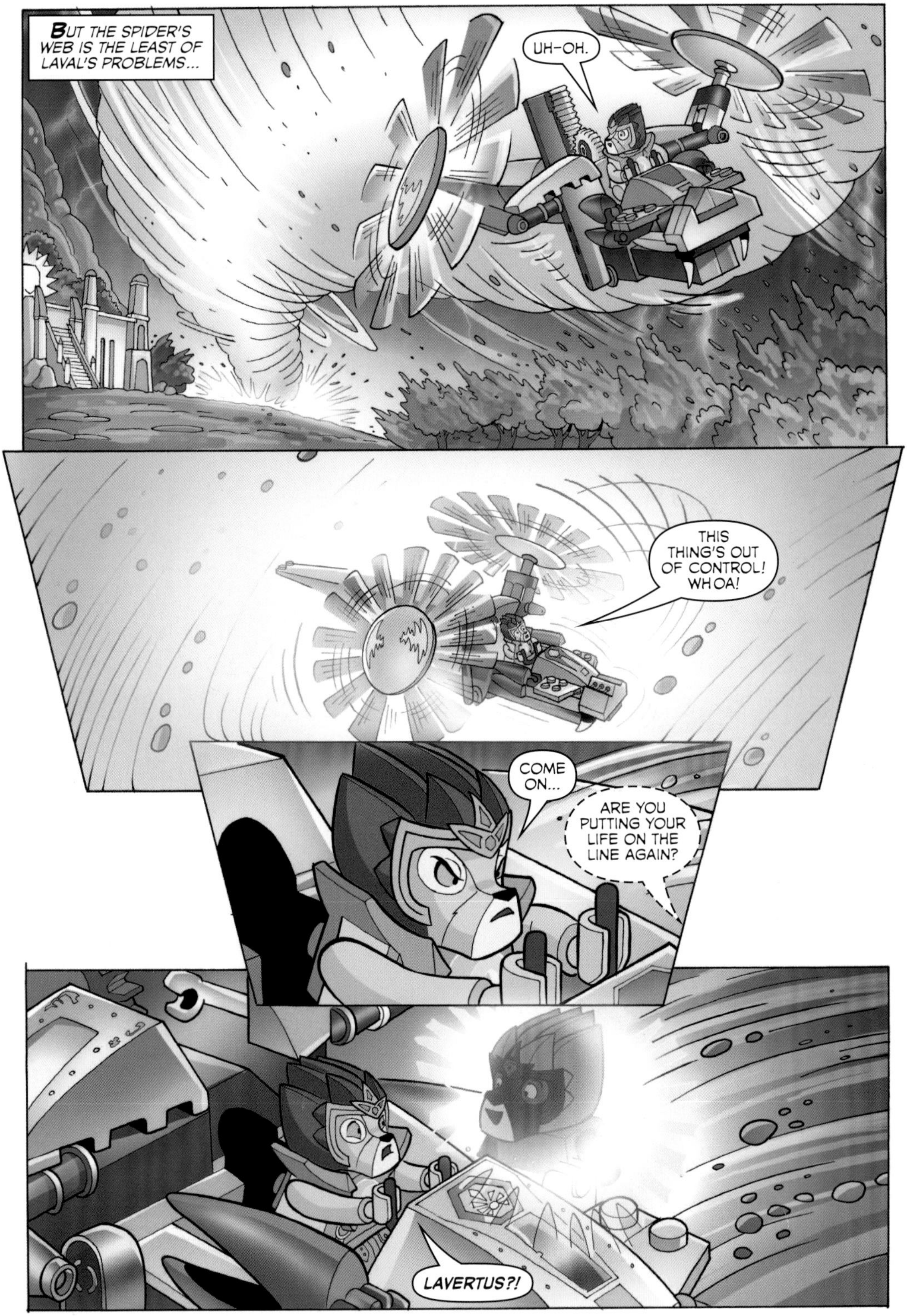
BUT THE SPIDER'S WEB IS THE LEAST OF LAVAL'S PROBLEMS...
UH-OH.
THIS THING'S OUT OF CONTROL! WHOA!
COME ON...
ARE YOU PUTTING YOUR LIFE ON THE LINE AGAIN?
LAVERTUS?!

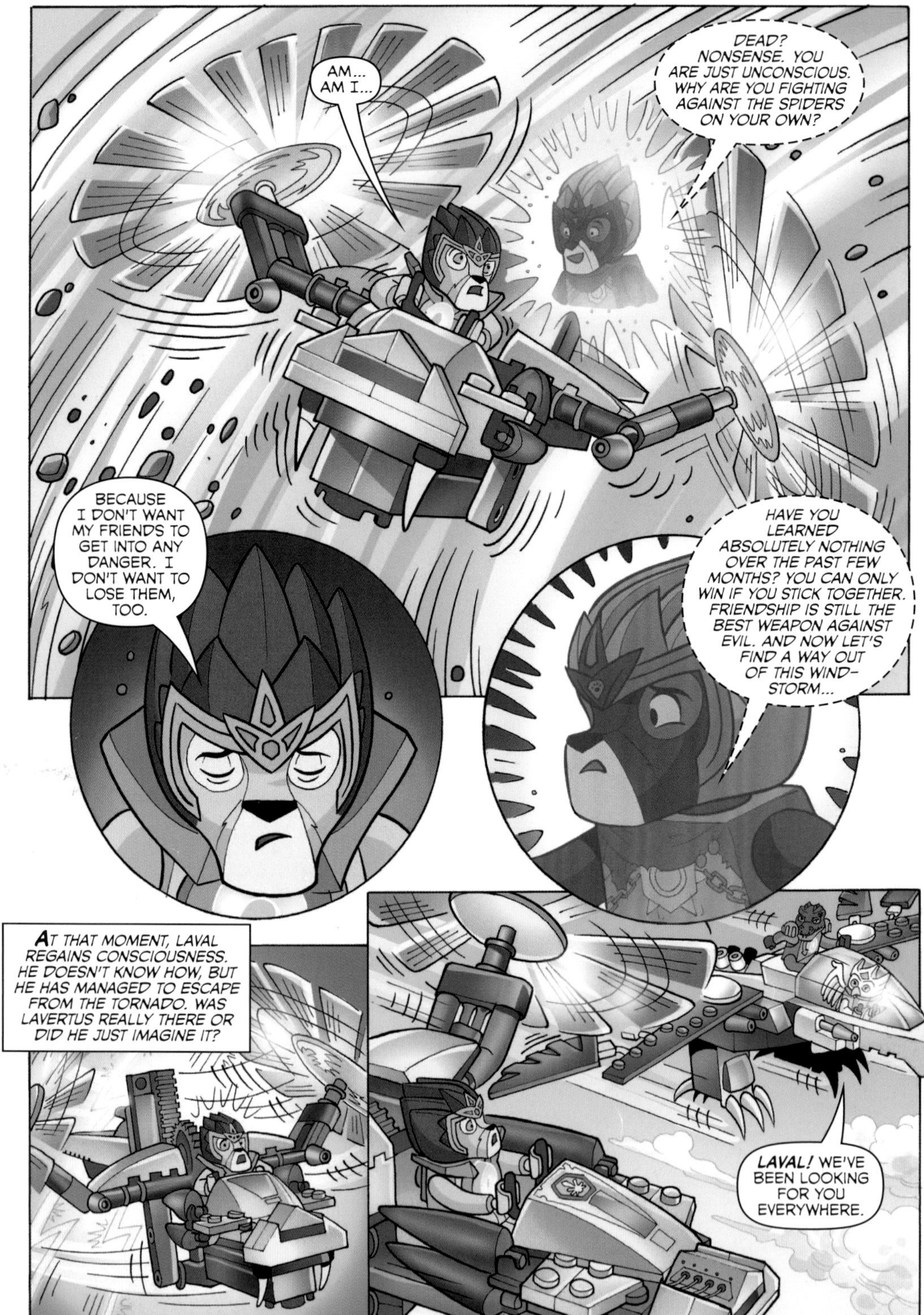
AM... AM I...
DEAD? NONSENSE. YOU ARE JUST UNCONSCIOUS. WHY ARE YOU FIGHTING AGAINST THE SPIDERS ON YOUR OWN?
BECAUSE I DON'T WANT MY FRIENDS TO GET INTO ANY DANGER. I DON'T WANT TO LOSE THEM, TOO.
HAVE YOU LEARNED ABSOLUTELY NOTHING OVER THE PAST FEW MONTHS? YOU CAN ONLY WIN IF YOU STICK TOGETHER. FRIENDSHIP IS STILL THE BEST WEAPON AGAINST EVIL. AND NOW LET'S FIND A WAY OUT OF THIS WIND-STORM...
AT THAT MOMENT, LAVAL REGAINS CONSCIOUSNESS. HE DOESN'T KNOW HOW, BUT HE HAS MANAGED TO ESCAPE FROM THE TORNADO. WAS LAVERTUS REALLY THERE OR DID HE JUST IMAGINE IT?
LAVAL! WE'VE BEEN LOOKING FOR YOU EVERYWHERE.

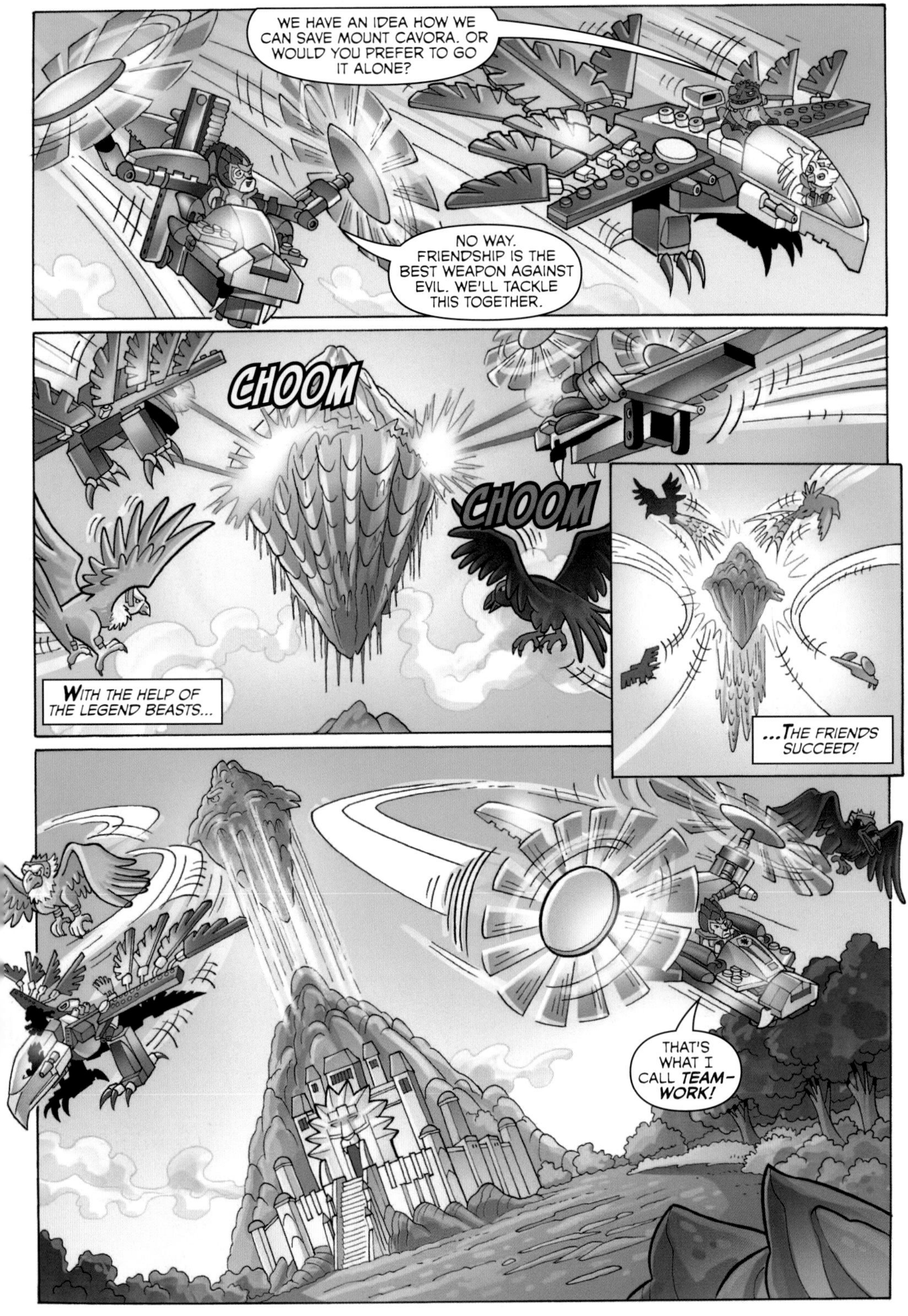
WE HAVE AN IDEA HOW WE CAN SAVE MOUNT CAVORA. OR WOULD YOU PREFER TO GO IT ALONE?
NO WAY. FRIENDSHIP IS THE BEST WEAPON AGAINST EVIL. WE'LL TACKLE THIS TOGETHER.
CHOOM
CHOOM
WITH THE HELP OF THE LEGEND BEASTS...
...THE FRIENDS SUCCEED!
THAT'S WHAT I CALL TEAM-WORK!

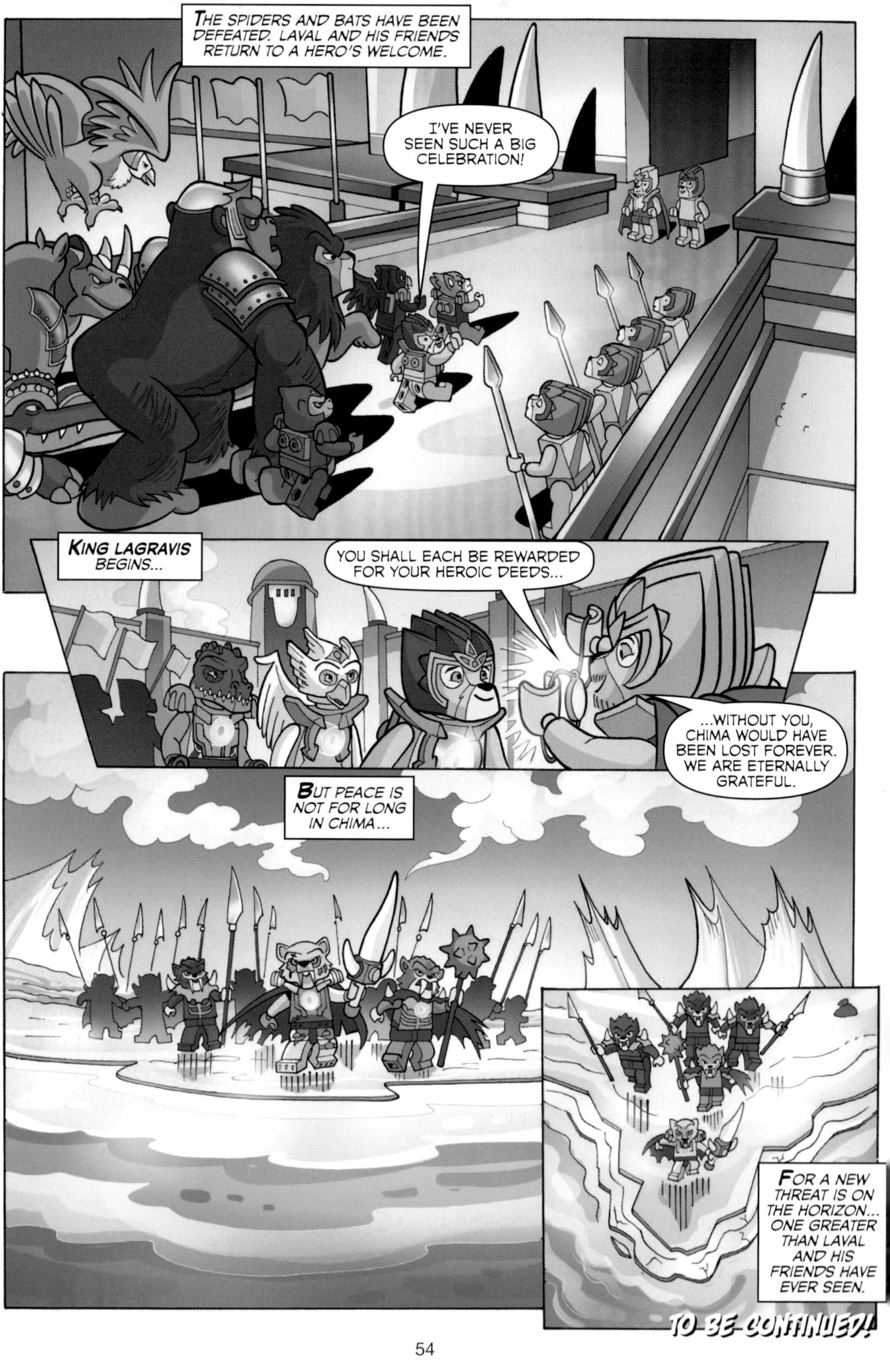
THE SPIDERS AND BATS HAVE BEEN DEFEATED. LAVAL AND HIS FRIENDS RETURN TO A HERO'S WELCOME.
I'VE NEVER SEEN SUCH A BIG CELEBRATION!
KING LAGRAVIS BEGINS...
YOU SHALL EACH BE REWARDED FOR YOUR HEROIC DEEDS...
...WITHOUT YOU, CHIMA WOULD HAVE BEEN LOST FOREVER. WE ARE ETERNALLY GRATEFUL.
BUT PEACE IS NOT FOR LONG IN CHIMA...
FOR A NEW THREAT IS ON THE HORIZON... ONE GREATER THAN LAVAL AND HIS FRIENDS HAVE EVER SEEN.
TO BE CONTINUED!

WATCH OUT FOR PAPERCUTZ

Welcome to the sensational second LEGO® LEGENDS OF CHIMA graphic novel, by Yannick Grotholt and Comicon, from Papercutz, those Chi-powered people dedicated to publishing great graphic novels for all ages. I'm Jim Salicrup, the Editor-in-Chief and Crooler's on-call beauty consultant. I'm here to offer up news, behind-the-scenes info, and sincere thanks. Let's start with the thanking...

My partner, Papercutz publisher Terry Nantier, and the entire hard-working staff of Papercutz and I want to express how grateful we are to you for your support of the LEGO LEGENDS OF CHIMA graphic novel series. Papercutz is just a teeny-tiny company, trying its very best to provide you with the kind of entertaining comics that you love, competing against countless competitors, many of them huge media corporations! And thanks to the wonderful folks at LEGO, we are fortunate enough to bring you the characters you love in all-new comics form. As a result, our very first LEGO LEGENDS OF CHIMA graphic novel was a big success—for which we thank you!

If this is actually your very first LEGO LEGENDS OF CHIMA graphic novel, we thank you for your support too! And don't worry—the collectors' item first graphic novel is still available at bookstores, comicbook stores, online booksellers, and us (see page 2). Just as most of the LEGO Group fans love collecting LEGO sets of their favorite characters, we know LEGO fans want to collect our graphic novels as well. Believe us—we know! We've had to break the news to frustrated LEGO fans more than once that certain hardcover editions of LEGO BIONICLE graphic novels are currently sold out.

As for news, be sure to mark your calendars—coming to a theater near you on September 23, 2016 is the all-new LEGO NINJAGO 3D movie! Yeah, we know—that seems so far away! But in the meantime, one of the most exciting events in the world of LEGO happens in the 10th LEGO NINJAGO graphic novel-- available right now! It's the dramatic debut of the Phantom Ninja! The only place you can find this exciting new Ninjago character is exclusively in the pages of NINJAGO #10 "The Phantom Ninja"! We're already getting bombarded at Papercutz with countless requests to create an all-new Phantom Ninja graphic novel series—fans are that excited about this new character! See for yourself what all the fuss is about—before the graphic novel sells out!

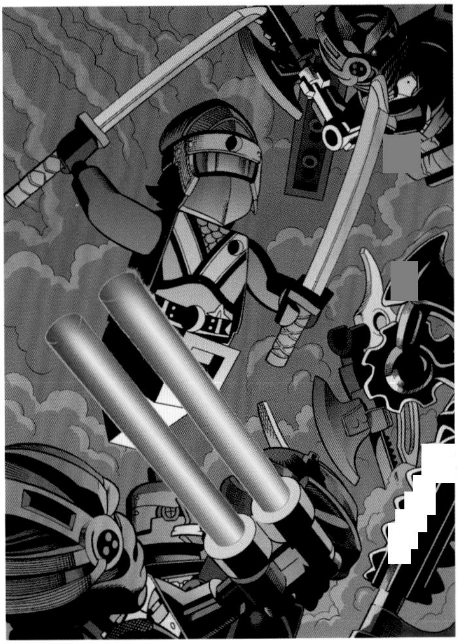

Finally, a little behind-the-scenes info. Many of you have wondered who this mysterious "Comicon," that was listed in the art credits in the premiere LEGO LEGENDS OF CHIMA graphic novel, might be. The answer is that it's the name of the comic art studio providing the stunning visuals for the actual comic art pages! Specifically, for LEGO LEGENDS OF CHIMA #1, it was: Miguel Sanchez, pencil art; Marc Alberich, ink art; and Oriol San Julian, color art. Together they are "Comicon" and they did a beautiful job illustrating Yannick Grotholt's scripts!

Speaking of which, don't miss Grotholt and Comicon's next collaboration in LEGO THE LEGENDS OF CHIMA #3 "CHI Quest!" coming soon!

Long Live Laval!

Thanks,

Jim

STAY IN TOUCH!

EMAIL:	salicrup@papercutz.com
WEB:	papercutz.com
TWITTER:	@papercutzgn
FACEBOOK:	PAPERCUTZGRAPHICNOVELS
FAN MAIL:	Papercutz, 160 Broadway, Suite 700, East Wing, New York, NY 10038

KIDS GO FREE

with full price adult ticket to LEGOLAND® Parks or LEGOLAND Discovery Centers

Purchase this offer at **LEGOLAND.com/LEGOPapercutz** now through 12/31/2015.

Offer good for one free one-day child ticket with purchase of a full-price one-day adult ticket to LEGOLAND® California, LEGOLAND Florida or LEGOLAND Discovery Centers. Valid for one complimentary child. Offer cannot be applied to pre-purchased, two day tickets, memberships, online ticket sales or combined with any other discounts or offers. No photocopies or facsimiles will be accepted. Additional restrictions may apply. Prices and hours subject to change without notice. The right of final interpretation resides with LEGOLAND. Not for resale. **Expires 12/31/2015.**
Discount ID 149930

LEGOLAND
DISCOVERY CENTER

Atlanta • Boston • Chicago • Dallas/Fort Worth
Kansas City • Toronto • Westchester

Indoor Attraction • LEGO Rides • LEGO MINILAND • 4D Cinema • LEGO Factory Tour • Play Zone • Birthday Room • Shop & Cafe